P9-APL-314

"My *dat* can be a handful…"

"I'm not worried about that." Jack pulled off his sunglasses to meet Beth's gaze. "I reckon he'd stay right here with us."

She eyed him suspiciously, trying to figure out why he was so set on her *dat* being here. Did he really want him or did he have some ulterior motive? "Why would you want to take responsibility for him? He's not your *dat*."

"Because he wants to be here." His grin was lazy. "And because I like you, Beth. I like doing something nice for a pretty girl like yourself."

Beth's mouth went dry and she stared at him for a moment, his comment taking her completely off guard.

Was he *flirting* with her?

She quickly looked away. She prided herself in being a person who always knew what to do and say in any situation, but not this time. Men as good-looking and confident as Jack didn't flirt with women like her. They flirted with girls like her sister. He couldn't possibly be interested in her.

Could he?

Emma Miller lives quietly in her old farmhouse in rural Delaware. Fortunate enough to have been born into a family of strong faith, she grew up on a dairy farm, surrounded by loving parents, siblings, grandparents, aunts, uncles and cousins. Emma was educated in local schools and once taught in an Amish schoolhouse. When she's not caring for her large family, reading and writing are her favorite pastimes.

Books by Emma Miller

Love Inspired

Seven Amish Sisters

Her Surprise Christmas Courtship
Falling for the Amish Bad Boy

The Amish Spinster's Courtship
The Christmas Courtship
A Summer Amish Courtship
An Amish Holiday Courtship
Courting His Amish Wife
Their Secret Courtship

The Amish Matchmaker

A Match for Addy
A Husband for Mari
A Beau for Katie
A Love for Leah
A Groom for Ruby
A Man for Honor

Visit the Author Profile page at LoveInspired.com for more titles.

Falling for the Amish Bad Boy

Emma Miller

LOVE INSPIRED
INSPIRATIONAL ROMANCE

If you purchased this book without a cover you should be aware that this book is stolen property. It was reported as "unsold and destroyed" to the publisher, and neither the author nor the publisher has received any payment for this "stripped book."

LOVE INSPIRED®
INSPIRATIONAL ROMANCE

Recycling programs
for this product may
not exist in your area.

ISBN-13: 978-1-335-58632-2

Falling for the Amish Bad Boy

Copyright © 2023 by Emma Miller

All rights reserved. No part of this book may be used or reproduced in any manner whatsoever without written permission except in the case of brief quotations embodied in critical articles and reviews.

This is a work of fiction. Names, characters, places and incidents are either the product of the author's imagination or are used fictitiously. Any resemblance to actual persons, living or dead, businesses, companies, events or locales is entirely coincidental.

For questions and comments about the quality of this book, please contact us at CustomerService@Harlequin.com.

Love Inspired
22 Adelaide St. West, 41st Floor
Toronto, Ontario M5H 4E3, Canada
www.LoveInspired.com

Printed in U.S.A.

With God all things are possible.
—*Matthew* 19:26

For Candace, a compeer and friend
who has become family.

Chapter One

Beth adjusted the reins in her gloved hands and eased out onto the blacktop road in the family wagon. Her father's mild-mannered driving horse lifted his velvety nose and took a deep breath of the fresh spring air as he fell into an easy trot.

"I'm glad you decided to come with me," Beth told her sister Willa, seated on the wooden bench beside her. "You needed to get out of the house and it's such a perfect day for a ride." She lifted her chin to enjoy the heat of the sun's rays. It had been raining for days, which was good for the soil but tiresome after a long winter. Spring was finally in the air, and Beth felt more alive than she had in a long time.

"*Ya*, it was time. I can't hide from Jack forever." Willa, the prettiest of her six sisters, chewed on her bottom lip. "I know that."

Taking the reins in one hand, Beth squeezed Willa's with the other. "He's not worth another moment of unhappiness. You know that, *ya*? It's time to put Jack Lehman behind you. It's a beautiful day, and there are as many boys out there waiting to walk out with you as blades of new grass."

Willa chuckled and glanced at the field across the street from their farm. Elden Yoder, betrothed to her twin sister, Millie, was pulling a plow behind his workhorse in the distance. He was too far away for them to call to him, but both sisters raised their hands in greeting and he waved back.

A gentle breeze ruffled tendrils of hair that had escaped Beth's black wool scarf she wore tied beneath her chin. She hadn't bothered to put on a white prayer *kapp* for their outing because they were only going to Raber's Seed & Feed store three miles from home. When they returned from fetching the chicken mash, she and Willa would mop every floor in their farmhouse. There was something about spring-cleaning that Beth always loved. Every year when the crocuses began to peek out of the soil in flower beds, around trees and alongside the road, she felt a renewed sense of well-being. "To everything there is a season." That's what the Bible said.

The last two years had been a season of sadness. Their mother had fallen ill with kidney disease and passed away. Around the same time, their *dat* was diagnosed with early-onset dementia, so in many ways, they lost him, too. Or rather they were losing him, one day at a time. As Beth and her sisters had ridden the waves of grief, they had clung together, reminding each other that it wasn't their place to question God's will. While they sought firm ground again, they tried to focus on all they had, not what they didn't have, and God's goodness was always the first of their thanksgivings. They simply needed time to adjust to the changes in their lives.

For Beth, however, it hadn't been until her sister Millie's romance with their handsome neighbor that she began to feel a lightness in her heart. And now, with the sun shining brightly on her face and the scent of freshly turned soil on the breeze, she was beginning to feel like herself again. For two years, she'd been going through the motions of being Beth Koffman, but she'd felt like a shadow of the girl she had been. It was as if she were watching herself go through the motions of life, but not living them. Now, at last, it seemed as if she was coming into a season of happiness. She didn't know what had given her this morning's sense of hope and joy in the simple things in life, but she didn't care.

"Jack isn't worth a tear, *schweschter*," Willa mused firmly. "I know he wasn't the man I thought he was. He isn't worth all this fuss." She picked at a piece of fuzz on her pristine white apron. Like Beth, she wore a homemade dress, a denim-cloth jacket and a scarf tied beneath her chin. Willa lifted her pert nose and sniffed. "I don't know what made me think he was a man I would want to marry. He'll be blessed if he ever finds a wife. Certainly not anyone in Honeycomb would have him. Not a cheater like him."

Beth slowed Joe, turned off their street onto Clover Road and passed an Amish schoolhouse.

"Not a cheater like him," she agreed.

When Willa broke up with Jack, no one in their family was surprised. They hadn't seemed to have much in common, and Jack had a reputation as a lady's man. In many of their elders' eyes, he'd dated far more young women than was appropriate. It wasn't the

Amish way, at least not the way it had been for hundreds of years. Their Old Order community encouraged young men and women of marrying age to meet and spend time together in groups, but with the intent of looking for a spouse. Couples were not supposed to date in the English way, but rather with the specific intention of marrying. When a single man and a single woman were seen together at multiple public events in Honeycomb, they were supposed to be either betrothed or about to announce their betrothal. And if a couple was dating, spending time with someone else was greatly frowned upon.

"Looks like Raber's is busy today," Willa observed.

Ahead, Beth spotted Raber's store, located on Jessop and Sissy Raber's farm. Like many Amish families in Kent County, as income from crops had dwindled, the Rabers sought other ways to care for their family financially. For them, opening their own feed business to sell to their Amish and English neighbors was even more successful than they'd thought possible. Three years ago, they'd been selling bags of grain out of an old chicken coop with a roof that leaked. But last year they'd been able to put up a building that was as nice as any feed-store in Dover.

Beth eased the wagon off the road and into the gravel parking lot with a skilled, gentle hand. Knowing it was a necessary skill for a female, her *dat* had taught all his daughters how to drive a horse and wagon from a young age. And while he respected the Amish way of traditional male and female roles, he'd always made it clear that, like their mother, they could do anything they put their mind to. With no sons to till his fields or run to the feedstore on an errand, his daughters had always done chores at his side, and he had always taken pride in their abilities.

There were several horse-drawn buggies and wagons in the parking lot along with three pickup trucks and a minivan. Careful not to disturb the other horses, Beth eased into a spot at the end of a long hitching post. "What do you think about running over to say hi to Rosie after we finish up here?" she asked her sister. She wanted to make Willa's first outing in weeks, except to go to church, an enjoyable one, but she didn't want to push her.

Rosie was Beth's Mennonite friend who lived near the Rabers. She had welcomed the idea of a neighborhood general store and had asked if they'd like to try selling her home-made ice cream there.

"When I saw Rosie at Byler's yesterday, she said she was working on new recipes. She wanted me to stop by and try some." Beth laughed. "She said she needs someone to eat the ice cream because she's running out of room for meat and vegetables in her freezer." When she looked at her sister, she could tell that Willa was contemplating the additional stop. "Rosie made waffle cones…" she said, trying to make the treat sound as tempting as possible. Willa loved ice cream cones. "I want to try the pistachio chocolate chunk."

Willa turned to Beth, her hands folded on her lap. "I suppose it's time I get back out of the house. I can't let Jack ruin my life." Her lower lip quivered and her brow furrowed as if she were about to cry. "Even if I did think he was going to marry me."

Beth squeezed her sister's hand again. "He's not worth another tear. You're far too good for him. Too pretty," she added, knowing that while vanity was not encouraged in their faith, Willa liked to be reminded of how attractive she was.

Willa flashed a smile. *"Oll recht."*

"All right?" Beth asked as she wrapped the

leather reins around the hand brake and swung her legs over to get down and tie up the horse.

"All right," Willa repeated with a firm nod. "Let's go see Rosie after we're done here and have some ice cream. And maybe we can take some home for *Dat*." She lowered herself from the wagon. "You know how much he loves chocolate ice cream. You think she has chocolate?"

Beth smiled at her sister as she walked beside her on the concrete sidewalk and headed for the steps that led to a loading platform that ran along the front of the newly constructed block building. "I know she does!"

As they made their way toward the door, Beth nodded to two elderly Amish brothers from their church district. They were seated on opposite sides of an old wooden barrel on the loading platform, a checkerboard on top. According to one of their granddaughters, the Zook brothers spent hours playing checkers there each day, which kept them out of trouble. "Amos. Bert." She nodded. In their eighties, both men were widowers and lived together in a *dawdi haus* on Amos's grandson's farm.

"Beth," Amos said. "Willa. How's your *dat* doing?" He spoke in Pennsylvania *Deitsch*, even though he could speak English like all the Amish in Honeycomb over the age of six. "You should bring him over to play checkers sometime."

Beth nodded. "*Ya*, maybe I will," she agreed, even though she doubted it would ever happen. Her father knew how to play checkers, but how long would it be before he couldn't? When he'd first been diagnosed, the family had thought he was just forgetful, but he suffered more bouts of confusion as time passed. His doctor said there was no way to predict how quickly his dementia would progress. They only knew that it would become worse.

Beth walked through the double doors left open to invite in the fragrant spring breeze. Not only did Jessop sell grain and hay but also a bit of everything one might need to run a farm and care for barnyard animals. He sold items like fencing, animal dewormer and even seeds for planting. There were rows and rows of neatly stocked shelves with various assorted items, and Beth always enjoyed coming in to see what was new in stock.

"I'll order the feed. You want to see if they've got any fly spray for the horses? *Dat* is worried about flies with the warmer weather coming and he doesn't want to see them suffer," Beth told Willa as she pointed down a row of shelves. "Halfway down, I think. Near the flea powder."

Beth and Willa split up, and Beth headed for the front counter. Besides the handful of customers walking around, there were three people in line ahead of her: two Amish men and an Englisher. She knew both Amish men and nodded to them. Both men returned with greetings.

"Guder mariye."

"Guder dawg."

She smiled at them and glanced at the checkout counter. Jessop Raber, who was about her father's age, was ringing up the Englisher's purchases and chatting as he dropped items into a plain brown paper bag. Beth was taking her place at the end of the line when, out of the corner of her eye, she spotted a young Amish man coming around the endcap of an aisle at the far side of the store. He looked enough like Jack Lehman that she did a double take.

Then she realized it *was* Jack Lehman.

"Willa!" Beth called, hurrying toward her sister. "Don't worry about the spray." She thought maybe she could get Willa back to the wagon before Jack and her sister saw each other. This was the first day Willa had left their farm of her own free will. Beth knew she wasn't ready to see him. "We can get it—"

"Willa," Jack called out.

Beth squeezed her eyes shut in disbelief. What were the chances Willa would have come to the feedstore at the exact moment as Jack?

Willa, who had a can of fly spray in her hand, looked up, wondering who had called her name. Not seeing Jack, she met Beth's gaze in apparent confusion.

"Come on." Beth waved to her. "Let's go."

"Go? But you didn't pay for the grain yet. I thought—" Then Willa saw him and let out a sound of surprise.

Willa clamped her hand on her mouth and turned and ran toward Beth. Beth took the spray can from her sister, set it on a shelf, threw her arm around her waist and hurried her out the door.

"What's *he* doing here?" Willa sobbed when they stepped out onto the loading dock.

The two elderly brothers playing checkers looked on in interest.

"It's *oll recht*," Beth assured her. "Let's go home."

Tears ran down Willa's face. "But *Dat* asked you to get the chicken feed. We can't go home without it."

"I'll get the feed tomorrow," Beth assured her, speaking in a soothing tone.

"I know I have to see him at some point."
Willa lowered her head, pulling a fresh handkerchief from her apron pocket to delicately
dab at her nose. Even when she cried, she was
pretty. "But not yet. Why is he here?" she blub-
bered. "Why is he following me?"

Beth turned her back to the Zook brothers,
blocking their view of Willa. She knew her sister wouldn't want anyone to see her this way.
"He's not following you. You haven't heard
from nor seen him in weeks. He must've
needed feed or something."

"Willa?" came Jack's tenor voice from inside the store. "Wait a minute. I want to talk
to you."

They spotted Jack through the open doors,
striding in their direction.

Her heart fluttering, Beth clasped Willa's
forearms and looked directly into her teary
eyes. "Go to the wagon. I'll get the feed." She
released her. "Wait in the wagon. I'll be right
there."

Willa hurried down the steps. At the same
time, Beth saw Lavinia Yoder come up the
walkway. She was Elden's mother and would
soon be their sister Millie's mother-in-law.
Of all the people walking into the store, she
was the last person Beth wanted to see. The

woman had a good heart, but she loved to gossip with her widowed friends. By church Sunday, everyone in Honeycomb would know that Jack and Willa had run into each other, and it wouldn't be too far-fetched to think there would be a lot of guesses as to what had transpired. Beth loved that their community was a close-knit one, but there were days when she longed for friends and neighbors who were a little less interested in everyone's lives.

"Willa!" Jack called again.

Willa's teary eyes widened as she gazed at Beth over her shoulder. "What about Jack?"

Beth set her jaw angrily. "I'll take care of him." Then she spun around and strode back through the door.

Jack was in such a hurry to catch Willa before she left that he almost ran smack into her sister in the doorway. Startled, he took an unbalanced step back and watched Willa rush down the steps. He looked at Beth.

Beth dropped her hands to her hips, blocking his way. She was wearing a rose-colored dress, and he noticed that the centers of her cheeks were the same hue. "What do you think you're doing?" she demanded.

"What?" he asked, instinctively taking a step back.

"You heard me!" Beth pointed an accusing finger. "You ought to be ashamed of yourself."

"Beth, please." He glanced around uncomfortably. The store was full of people. "Lower your voice."

"You cheated on my sister!" she responded even louder.

He frowned, drawing back. "I did not—"

"I knew she should never have walked out with you," Beth went on, taking a step toward him. "Everyone in Honeycomb knows you're not to be trusted."

He took another step back, staring at her. That was such an awful thing to hear that he didn't know how to respond.

But Beth didn't wait for an answer. "Don't talk to her. Ever again." She pointed once more. "Don't even look at her!"

He watched with disappointment as Willa disappeared from his sight around the corner of the building. It upset him that Willa felt like she should have to run from him. He hadn't wanted their relationship to end this way. All he wanted to do was to make sure she was all right. He hadn't seen her in weeks, not since their breakup. *Our second breakup.*

Pushing the brim of his straw hat up, Jack returned his gaze to Beth. He didn't know her well. She was as pretty as the other Koffman girls, though some might say not as pretty as Willa. There was something sturdy about Beth and...intimidating. That was the word. "Beth, I only want to make sure she's okay. We didn't part on the best of terms—"

"*You think*?" Beth interrupted. She narrowed her gaze angrily. "How could you hurt her like that? She cared for you. She *trusted* you."

Jack still wasn't sure what to say. Obviously, the Koffman family had a different notion of what happened between him and Willa than what actually happened. His first impulse was to tell Beth that she didn't know what she was talking about. But he thought better of it, out of respect for Willa. What had passed between them was private, wasn't it? Unless Willa chose to share.

"Well?" Beth demanded. "If you have something to say, say it. Otherwise, step out of my way."

"You're the one in my way," Jack accused. Then he saw Lavinia Yoder dressed head to toe in a black cloak and bonnet coming up behind Beth and groaned. Of all the people to overhear this conversation. He reached out to touch Beth's shoulder to move her aside, afraid that Lavinia would bowl them both over in her eagerness to see what was going on.

"Don't touch me!" Beth flared, swatting at him.

"Jack," Lavinia said.

Jack nodded and Beth swung around, startled. "Lavinia."

Lavinia was a widow who lived across the street from the Koffmans. Her only son, Elden, would marry Beth's and Willa's sister Millie in a few months.

The tall, slender woman looked from Jack to Beth, then back to Jack. "Everything all right here?"

"Fine," Jack managed, embarrassed that Beth was making such a fuss in front of people they knew. He felt like everyone in the shop was staring at them. Both Zook brothers had gotten off their stools, where he thought they were permanent fixtures, and stood side by side, watching them intently.

"Beth?" The widow looked down her long, sloping nose.

Beth drew a tight-lipped smile. "*Goot*," she murmured. "We're *goot* here, Lavinia."

The older woman lifted her gaze, obviously looking at something or someone. Jack turned around to see that the customers waiting in line near the front counter were staring at them. The owner, Jessop Raber, had stopped bagging for an Englisher in a ball cap and was watching, too. Jack turned back to the women, looking at Beth who, unlike Willa, was tall enough that he could gaze directly into her eyes.

Beth gritted her teeth seeming to keep her ire barely in check. "Jack and I were just talking."

Lavinia circled them, staring as she passed. "Were you, then? I would ask about what, but you know me, I mind my own knitting. Of course it doesn't take much to put two and two together, what with Willa and her waterworks."

Neither Jack nor Beth responded.

Seeming disappointed, Lavinia walked away, and Beth met Jack's gaze again. "Now look what you've done. She'll tell everyone in the county about this."

"Me?" He touched his chest between the straps of his leather suspenders. "I'm the innocent one here. I just came to get some radish seeds for my mother."

"And made my sister cry!"

"I did not—" Jack caught himself when he realized he had raised his voice. He didn't want to be that kind of man. Not ever. What was it about these Koffman girls that made him behave poorly? He knew he hadn't handled his relationship with Willa well, and he regretted it. All he wanted to do was to tell Willa that he was sorry. And now here Beth was, putting herself in the middle of it.

"Stay away from her," Beth hissed, leaning closer to him. "If you see her, walk away." She gestured broadly and turned around to go.

"Beth, you're not listening to me." Jack didn't know what had possessed him, but he followed her onto the loading dock. "I only want to talk to her. To make sure she's all right. That *we're* all right. I didn't mean to hurt her. I—"

"Who's the one who's not listening now?" Beth asked, swinging back to face him. "What do you not understand? She doesn't want to talk to you."

The Zook brothers now stood close enough that there wasn't any way they couldn't hear every word that was said.

"She doesn't want to see you again. Ever," Beth said firmly. She started down the concrete steps and then threw over her shoulder, "And neither do I, Jack Lehman!"

Jack just stood there, dumbfounded as he watched Beth stride away. How had he got himself into these kinds of situations with girls?

"Which one?"

The question startled Jack and he looked at the Zook brothers. "What?"

Amos, the older of the two, crossed his arms over his hollow chest and leaned back thoughtfully. "That's what Bert and I are wondering."

Jack frowned. He had no idea what Amos was talking about. "Which one what?"

Amos shot a look at his brother and flashed a toothless smile. "Which one of the Koffman girls are you going to marry? I got my eye on the pretty little one, but Bert says it will be the tall, loudmouthed one."

The older men cackled with laughter, and Jack walked down the steps without his mother's radish seeds.

Chapter Two

The horse and wagon had barely rolled to a stop in the barnyard when Willa jumped out and hurried toward the front porch of their white clapboard farmhouse. There, Eleanor was sweeping and Jane, their youngest sister at nearly seventeen, was weeding their mother's flower bed. Henrietta, in a pair of their father's breeches beneath her green dress, stood on a ladder, replacing shingles that had come loose on the porch roof.

"You're not going to believe who we ran into at Raber's," Willa called to them.

Beth watched Willa go, glad her sister had recovered from her encounter with Jack. Beth hadn't. She was still upset, oddly even more upset than Willa. But Willa was always one for a bucket of tears that could turn into laughter in a moment.

"Who?" Jane asked, coming to her feet. She dusted dark, rich soil from her hands by rubbing them together. "I knew I should have gone with you." She shot Eleanor a look. Jane had wanted to go to the feedstore, too, but their eldest sister had insisted she stay home to help with chores. Jane was at that age when she desperately wanted more social interaction and was always up to go anywhere or do anything, even it was to walk to a neighbor's farm to deliver cookies.

As Beth took their horse by his halter, Cora came out of the barn, their father trailing her. He wore his good black felt hat meant only for church Sunday, but Beth didn't say anything.

When he'd first begun to experience memory loss and odd behavior, they'd assumed it was because their mother was dying and he was overwhelmed. They'd gently reminded him of things he'd forgotten or was supposed to do in those days. But after their mother's death and his diagnosis of early-onset dementia, they'd learned to choose carefully when to speak and when to hold their tongue. Nowadays, his safety was their priority, and after that, the rules got a bit murky, often depending on which sister was keeping an eye on him.

Cora let him wear or eat whatever he wanted, but she was a stickler for making sure he was groomed properly, which included daily shaving. Amish men did not have mustaches, and Cora wouldn't tolerate one. On the other hand, Beth didn't mind if his beard got a bit unruly or he had the shadow of a mustache, but she wouldn't let him eat as many cookies as he wanted, no matter how hard he begged. His doctor had warned them that he was a borderline diabetic, which meant he needed to limit his sweets and carbohydrates.

"Back already?" Cora asked. "I thought you would see Rosie after you picked up the feed. We were hoping you'd bring some ice cream home, weren't we, *Dadi*?"

He didn't respond.

"*Ya*, we were going to go," Beth said, "but then—" She exhaled, as annoyed with herself as she was with Jack Lehman. Why had she let him rile her like that in front of all those folks at the feedstore? Before the day was over, how many times would Lavinia repeat what Beth had said to him? "We ran into Jack," she said, lowering her voice.

"Don't see chicken mash." Their father

walked around to the back of the wagon. "And where's the cracked corn?"

"No cracked corn or mash today, *Dadi*. I'll go back tomorrow," Cora said, then she returned her attention to Beth.

"He wanted to talk to Willa, but she got upset." Beth worked her jaw, embarrassed now by her behavior. Well, maybe more regretful than embarrassed. "And then I sort of got into it with him."

"Where's the cracked corn?" their *dat* repeated, louder this time. It was something he did all the time. If he didn't get the response he wanted, he'd simply repeat himself louder.

"We didn't need cracked corn," Cora told him. She looked back at Beth, crossing her arms over her chest. "Got into it with him? Why? What did he say to Willa?"

Beth worked her jaw. "He didn't say anything," she admitted. "She ran outside when she saw him. She didn't want to talk to him."

Cora arched her brows. "So..." She drew out the word. "Willa didn't feel the need to talk to Jack, but *you* did?"

Beth nodded.

"And you *got into it* with him?" Cora asked using Beth's words. She stared at her through her wire-framed eyeglasses. "I don't understand."

"I sent you girls for cracked corn and instead you got mash," their father muttered, lifting one of the bags of feed from the back of the wagon to his shoulder. While his mind may have weakened, his strength hadn't. "That'll teach me to send you girls. I'll go myself next time."

Beth watched him carry the feed into the barn. It needed to go into the chicken coop, but she'd move it later. "He made Willa cry," she explained to her sister. "And I got mad. Because he hurt her. He cheated on her and he hurt her feelings terribly. What kind of man does that? Willa thought he was going to ask her to marry him."

Cora frowned. "He shouldn't have cheated on her, but he wasn't going to ask her to marry him. They weren't a good match."

Beth didn't know whether Jack had intended to ask Willa to be his wife, but did that matter? Willa thought he would.

Cora contemplated a moment. "Well, nothing to be done about it now." She walked around to grab Joe's halter. "I'll unhitch him for you. Get *Dat* to help. His hands always remember how to do it, even when his mind doesn't." She reached out and brushed Beth's arm. "You could always apologize next time you see Jack."

Beth narrowed her gaze. "I am not apologizing."

Cora chuckled as she led the horse and wagon away. Beth crossed the barnyard. Willa was standing at the foot of the porch steps, telling their sisters how Beth had kept Jack from going after her and what Beth had said to him.

"How did you know what I said?" Beth asked with surprise. "You went to the wagon."

"I could still hear you." Willa turned back to Jane, who was listening in rapt attention. "Beth told him to stay away from me," she went on as if it was the most exciting thing that had ever happened to her. "She told him he wasn't allowed to talk to me."

Nay, she didn't." Jane looked at Beth excitedly. "You were brave to take up for Willa."

Beth exhaled from the foot of the steps. "*Foolhardy* is more like it. Lavinia was there and she heard every word."

"And now everyone in Honeycomb will know about it," Henry called down from the ladder, punctuating her words with the bang of her hammer.

"Oh, dear," Eleanor said with a sigh. She

had been sweeping cobwebs from the porch ceiling but lowered her broom. "I suppose that means I'll hear about it. You know how Lavinia likes to tell me how we ought to behave." She frowned. "How you all ought to behave. How I should make you behave." She chuckled. "As if anyone could make any of the Koffman girls do anything."

"I'm sorry," Beth said, truly sorry if she'd made trouble for Eleanor. "It just sort of happened." She climbed the steps that needed painting. "But Willa was so upset, and that Jack, he had it coming to him." She stopped in front of Eleanor. "I don't think we should have anything else to do with him."

Eleanor arched an eyebrow and continued to sweep.

"It's time to stop tolerating that kind of behavior with these young men. They think girls are so desperate to marry them that they can behave any way they please!" As she spoke, Beth could feel her face growing warm as anger tightened in her chest. "If we continue to let them act this way without consequences, their behavior will never change."

A cobweb drifted downward, lighting on Eleanor's headscarf and she absently brushed it off.

"I don't think he should be welcome here and…and we shouldn't be talking to him," Beth continued. "Otherwise, next you know, he'll be trying to charm her." She lifted her chin in Jane's direction.

Eleanor's mouth twitched as if she was trying not to smile. "So you've taken it on yourself to decide who in our community should be shunned?"

Beth frowned, feeling that her big sister wasn't taking this whole thing seriously enough. "*Nay*, I'm not saying he should be shunned, *schweschter*. I'm saying…we, the Koffmans, shouldn't be talking to him. We should have nothing more to do with him."

"I'm not sure that would be too easy," Eleanor responded.

"I know." Beth began to pace the squeaky floorboards, raising her voice to be heard above Henry's banging overhead. "We've known him since we were children. *Mam* and *Dat* were friends with Sharar and Maree, but don't we owe it to other single women to stand up to men like him?"

"You don't think we should talk to Jack?" Eleanor repeated.

Beth crossed her arms over her chest with a nod.

"Well, that would be interesting." Eleanor knocked down an old wasp nest and it fell at her feet. "Seeing as how Monday morning he's going to start on the foundation for our store."

"What?" Beth demanded. "You hired him to build our store?"

"I did."

"This is the first I've heard of it," Beth said, her ire rising again.

Eleanor began to sweep again, pushing the papery nest into the pile of cobwebs. "Well, Beth, it gets tiresome having to repeat every decision I make six times. I was going to tell everyone at supper. He gave me the best out of four estimates. I'm sure he bid low because he's just getting his business up and running, but he was the only one who took the time to cost out the price of renovating one of our outbuildings instead of building a new one. And he pointed out that building on the road will bring us more business, especially from Englishers who might be hesitant to come up a private lane."

Beth stood there, stunned. "You hired Jack Lehman to build the store. Here. On our property? Knowing what he did to Willa."

Eleanor raised her brows, nodding. "With us being his only job, he says he can have it done in four months. No one else could promise its completion before winter. Everyone's busy."

"*Nay*," Beth said, shaking her head. "He cannot be here. He can't be the one."

"Well, he is." Eleanor pointed to the dustpan balanced on the rail of the open porch. "Would you grab that?"

Beth picked up the dustpan and placed it where her sister could sweep the pile of debris into it. "No," she repeated. "I don't want him here. Willa certainly doesn't want him here either."

"It's got to be him, Beth." Eleanor sounded impatient now. "I already signed the contract."

"Then unsign it." Beth tapped her sister's shoe and Eleanor took a step back.

Eleanor had been born with a congenital malformation of her foot, which had been amputated. She wore a prosthetic that wasn't visible beneath her skirt.

"I'm not breaking the contract." Eleanor took the dustpan from Beth. "Not only because it's wrong to break an agreement—" she strode to the screen door "—but we can't afford the price everyone else was asking."

Beth reached around her sister to open the door for her.

Eleanor carried the broom and dustpan into

the mudroom and dumped the cobwebs into a trash can. "We've got to get the store up and running as soon as possible." She hung the broom and dustpan next to a mop. "I try not to worry you girls, but with *Dat* no longer able to work, we need the income, Beth."

"I know," Beth said, following her into the kitchen. The wide bay of windows that overlooked the front porch was open, and a breeze drifted through, bringing in the scent of new grass. "But maybe someone else would be willing to come down in their price. Or…or… I don't know. Take payments?"

Eleanor began to pull leftovers from the refrigerator. On weekends, they ate their largest meal of the day around one o'clock, the traditional time for dinner. But during the week, they ate like Englishers, having a sandwich or whatever was left over from the big meal the day before. "*Dat* never in his life took out a loan." Eleanor's voice quivered. "And I'm not doing it now."

"It wouldn't exactly be a loan." Beth followed her to the counter. "We'd just be paying late. But each month on what we owe."

"*Nay*," Eleanor said firmly, popping the lids off plastic and glass storage containers. "I've thought about this for months, and I can't think about it anymore. I made my decision and Jack Lehman is the one who is going to build our store."

"But, Eleanor—"

"You know what," Eleanor interrupted. "Why don't you take over?"

Beth took a step back. Eleanor was the most patient one in the household; she never snapped at them. "What?"

"You heard me. You take over." She dumped some leftover chicken rice soup into a saucepan. "If you think you can do a better job, *you* be the one in charge of getting this store built. Then you can lie awake at night worrying about it."

Beth was immediately contrite. "Ellie, I wasn't saying you're not doing a good job, I just… Jack Lehman shouldn't be—" She cut herself off, realizing she was only making things worse. "I'm sorry." She clasped her hands together. "I wasn't criticizing you. You work so hard and take such good care of us. *Mam* would be proud of you. I know she's there in heaven, looking down on us."

Eleanor set the saucepan on the large propane gas stove and turned back to Beth. The two sisters looked at each other and Eleanor's face softened.

"I know you don't mean to be critical," Eleanor said, her voice gentle. "And I know you're just trying to look out for Willa, but you should take over this whole business of the store." She sighed, her hands falling to her sides. "I have so much going on, what with *Dat*—" she pointed in the direction of the barnyard "—and Millie's wedding to plan. November will be here before we know it and we've rooms to paint and Millie's hope chest to fill and—" She met Beth's gaze. "And you have been the one who's seen this plan clearly from the beginning." She lifted her hand and let it fall. "The store was your idea and it's a good idea. And I know we can make it work because you'll make it work."

Beth didn't know what to say. She was a middle sister. She'd never been in charge of anything in her life. First, her *mam* had told her what to do, then Eleanor.

Could she do it?

Could she oversee the building of their store?

Beth chewed on her lower lip. "I don't know anything about construction."

"And you think I do?" Eleanor laughed and went back to the counter. "Beth, that's why we hired a contractor. We don't have to know how to do it. We just have to make sure it gets done." She unwrapped a plate of leftover fried chicken. "So it's settled." She looked over her shoulder at Beth. "You'll see to the build. You'll keep Jack straight."

Beth hesitated for a long moment and said, "*Ya*, I'll do it. If that's what you need me to do." She pressed a hand to her forehead, unable to believe she'd just agreed to such a thing.

She was going to be Jack Lehman's boss.

On the day construction on the store began, Beth rose earlier than she usually would and watched the sunrise through the bank of kitchen windows as she started breakfast. When the family joined her in the kitchen, they shared freshly baked pumpkin muffins, fried scrapple and big, fluffy omelets. While Beth often enjoyed a casual cup of coffee with her sisters after breakfast, today she was the first to clear her plate and begin cleanup.

"You're in a hurry this morning," Henry said setting her dirty plate on the counter. "What are you up to?"

Beth scrubbed a cast-iron frying pan that had been a wedding gift to their mother thirty years ago. "The excavation for the foundation starts today." She stole a glance in Willa's direction, but Willa was deep in discussion with

Jane about a community barn raising. "I think it's wise that I make it clear to Jack Lehman that I'll have my eye on him and he'd better stay on the straight and narrow."

Henry walked to the refrigerator and pulled out the sack lunch she'd packed for herself the night before. "I have no doubt he will, with you constantly looking over his shoulder."

Beth sighed as she slid the wet frying pan into the warm oven to dry. She was having second thoughts about taking charge. She'd agreed to Eleanor's proposal the other day because she felt terrible that Elly had read her concerns as criticism, but now Beth wondered if it had been a mistake. What did she know about construction? About getting workmen to do what needed doing? "Would you rather do it?"

Henry wrinkled her nose. "Check up on Jack? No way."

"But you know something about construction."

Henry shook her head. "I don't."

"I know something about construction," their father said as he brought his mug to the stove for another cup of coffee.

Beth refilled his cup while still talking to Henry. "You can fix anything."

"Exactly. I know about repairs, not new construction." Henry peered into her lunch sack, then added a banana from a bowl on a baker's rack.

"Laid many a foundation in my day." Their father slurped his coffee loudly. "I was a mason. Did a little construction, too. I helped Elden's father build that house." He pointed in the direction of Millie's betrothed's property across the street. "Well, I best get ready for my day. Fine breakfast, daughters," he said, carrying his coffee out of the kitchen. "Your mother will be pleased to hear how good you feed me."

Henry and Beth watched him leave the kitchen, then Beth said, "Are you sure you wouldn't like to give it a try? At least you know something about building things. I don't know anything."

"I don't want to be anyone's boss." Henry headed for the mudroom. "I just want to work." Then she raised her voice so everyone would hear her, "I might not be home until supper."

"Where are you going again?" Eleanor asked, taking her dish to the sink.

"Sadie's," Henry said from the doorway.

Sadie Lapp, a woman in her.

midseventies from their church, had recently been widowed and struggled to keep up with their rambling farmhouse. It seemed like every other week she was asking Henry to repair something.

"She's got a leaky faucet, a window that won't open, a loose tile in the bathroom and I don't know what else," Henry said from the doorway. "I don't know how long it will take me."

"Stay as long as you need. Sit with her, if she invites you," Eleanor advised, going back to the table to remove the serving platters. "She may need a tender ear as much as a faucet that doesn't leak."

"*Ya,* I know," Henry answered. "I'm taking the wagon and Joe if I need to run into Dover for supplies."

"Wait," Willa called, popping up from the table. "I was going to take the buggy. Jane and I are going into Byler's to get bananas and more flour to make banana bread. Rosie said she and her *mam* could probably sell two dozen of our mini loaves at Spence's come Friday. If we don't get the bananas today, they won't be ripe enough to make the bread on Thursday."

Henry looked to Eleanor because Eleanor had the final word in such matters although she was their sister and not their mother.

"Take the wagon, Henry, but harness Bessie. Willa and Jane can take the buggy with Joe."

Henry scowled because she didn't get her way. "Fine. See everyone for supper."

Beth glanced at the kitchen wall clock. "Oh, my, I need to get going! I don't know what time Jack plans to start work, but I want to be there when he breaks ground to be sure he's in the right place. I want to make sure there's room for parking in the front and alongside the store, and Elden said that the county is picky about the right-of-ways." As she pulled off her dirty kitchen apron, she remembered she was still in her nightgown. "Oh! I have to get dressed still."

Eleanor took the apron from Beth and dropped it over her head. "Go. I'll take care of this. Cora can help me."

"Can't," Cora said, stuffing a last bit of muffin into her mouth as she carried her plate to the sink. "I told Aunt Judy I'd help her with her household budget. I guess Uncle Cyrus is too busy to do it these days with all of his duties as a new bishop."

"I'll help," Millie offered cheerfully, rising from the table. "Go, Beth." She giggled. "And let Jack know you're the boss."

Beth closed her eyes, praying silently that God would guide her in her task before she hurried upstairs to wash and dress.

Half an hour later, Beth buttoned her denim barn coat, stepped into black rubber boots because it had rained overnight and walked out onto the back porch. She was surprised to see her father sitting on the steps. She had assumed he was inside. "Whatcha doin', *Dat?*" she asked as she tied a black scarf securely under her chin.

He was sitting with his eyes closed, his face tilted upward toward the sky. "Sun's out," he told her.

She grabbed a newel post and glanced up. "*Ya*, it is." She glanced at the mud puddles in the barnyard. "Looks like we got a nice rain. It will be good for the garden."

"Sit with me, Beth," he said, his eyes still closed. He tapped the stair tread.

"Um…" She looked in the direction of the plot of land on the road where they were building the store. Because it was hard to see through a windbreak of trees, she couldn't tell if Jack and his crew had arrived yet. It was five after seven. She certainly expected them to be there. "I have an errand to run. They're starting work on the store today. Digging the foundation and I want to see how it's going."

"Sit, *dochtah*." He opened his eyes and looked at her. He'd significantly aged since their mother died. He was only sixty-one, but he looked ten years older. He still had a full head of hair but it had prematurely turned snow-white, as had his full beard. And there were lines around his mouth and eyes that she hadn't remembered seeing before her *mam* fell ill. "Sit," he repeated.

She thought of the many times she must have kept him from a task in the last twenty-three years, asking him to do the things a girl asked of her father, and sat down beside him. She tamped down her impatience to get to the building site and looked into his faded gray eyes. "It is nice here in the sun, isn't it?"

"You have to close your eyes." He clasped her hand with his knotty one and closed his eyes again. "Feel that?"

She did as he asked and breathed deeply, letting the sun's warmth fall on her face.

"That's *God*'s grace," he told her. "Can you feel it? That's what your *mam* told me before she died. She said that whenever I was lonely, all I needed to do was lift my face to the sky and feel His warmth. His love for us. And her love for me," he added, his gravelly voice catching in his throat.

Tears gathered suddenly in the corners of Beth's eyes and she gave a laugh that was half sadness, half joy. He was right; the sun did feel so good. It reminded her of how blessed she was, not only by *Gott*'s love, but the love of her family, her friends and her community.

"Feel it?" he asked.

"I do, *Dadi*." She took another deep breath, letting the warmth soak through her coat and envelop her, and she said a silent prayer of thanks for it.

They sat there for several minutes, side by side, eyes closed just being in the moment with each other, and then her father slapped his thighs and stood. "Well, best I get going."

Beth rose. "Where are you going?" For a few moments, he had seemed like the father she had known her whole life, the man she had known before his dementia diagnosis. And now that man was gone. That was one of the hardest things for her to deal with: the way his mind came and went with no warning.

He picked up a leather tool bag that had to be older than she was. "To work, of course." He tugged on the brim of his straw hat. "You forget we're building a store. Calling it Koffman's. Not catchy." He went down the walk. "But people will call it that anyway, so no sense wasting time coming up with a fancy name."

She followed him into the barnyard. "*Dat*, you're not building the store." She looked over her shoulder, trying to remember whose turn it was to keep an eye on him. Jane's maybe? All she knew was that today was not her day. "We hired a contractor. Remember?"

He kept walking. "Not going to get built on its own. See, first you stake out the foundation, then you start digging. I hope your *mam* put my lunch in my tool bag. She always packs my lunch when I go to work. I hope there are cookies. The ones with raisins."

"*Dat*, you don't have to put the foundation in. Jack Lehman will do it. He's who we hired. He brought his own crew." She darted ahead of him and stopped to face him. "You need to stay here."

He stared at her for a minute, and then his face fell. "I'm not going to work on my own store?" He stared at the muddy ground and she realized for the first time that he was dressed appropriately for once. He looked like a mason headed out to work for the day.

Beth felt terrible. "You…you don't have to work anymore," she said, trying to soften the blow. "You worked for so many years, *Dat*. Since you were fifteen, and…and now you can sit back and enjoy your life."

He stared straight ahead but his eyes weren't focused. "I don't work anymore," he repeated, sounding lost. "Your mother is gone and I don't work. Makes me wonder why I'm still here."

For a moment, she was afraid he might cry. But then he seemed to snap out of his thoughts, and he walked around her. "Ridiculous," he said. "This is my farm, that's my store and that's that." He took several long strides and then glanced back at her. "You coming or not?"

Beth closed her eyes in frustration. It was bad enough that she would have to deal with Jack, but having her father with her would make matters even worse. What if he actually tried to help?

"Not coming?" her father said. He headed down their lane. "Suit yourself."

"Wait, *Dat*!" Beth cried. "Wait for me." And then—because what choice did she have?—she hurried after him.

Chapter Three

When Jack saw Beth Koffman striding in his direction, it was obvious she was still madder than a wet hen with him. His first impulse was to run. That thought amused him and troubled him at the same time. Ordinarily, he wasn't a coward and he had never been shy with the ladies, but this one… She scared him right to his boots. No one had given him a dressing-down like Beth had since the widow Agnes Lapp when he was twelve. Agnes hadn't approved of the twenty-three toads he'd put in her buggy while she was having coffee with his mother. The widow had made him carry one toad at a time to safety while berating him in front of his friends. The event had been so scarring that he avoided toads to this day.

But Jack knew he couldn't run from Beth.

Where was he going to run *to*? There was no place to hide. The building wasn't up yet, and it was too far to reach the shade trees the Koffmans had wisely chosen to keep on the lot they'd had cleared for their store. So, Jack would have to face Beth—and pretend that she didn't intimidate him.

He watched her as she walked toward him, turning her head to speak with her *dat* at her side. Scary or not, he had to admire her devotion to her *vadder*. Her patience and kindness seemed to be without limits when it came to him. It was difficult for the tight-knit community of Honeycomb to watch Felty Koffman's mental decline, so he could only imagine what it was like for the man's daughters. First, the seven Koffman sisters had lost their mother, who had only been in her late forties, and then for this to happen to their father? God's ways were sometimes hard to understand. Even harder to accept, though he strived each day to do so.

Jack continued to observe Beth. She wasn't turn-around-to-gawk gorgeous like her sister Willa, but Beth was attractive, in a different way. She had silky blond hair, bright blue eyes and a slender figure that was less rounded than Willa's. There was something about Beth that was more than being physically attractive. It was the way she carried herself. It wasn't an air of conceit he saw in her stride but one of confidence. He admired that about her, wishing he had a bit more of it.

Beth caught Jack's eye and again the urge to flee came upon him. He brushed it aside because she was too close for him to hightail it out of there. Instead, he flashed a grin—the kind females, five to a hundred and five, were unable to resist.

The look Beth shot back as she approached him suggested she *could* resist. Easily.

Jack swallowed. "Beth. Felty." He tugged on the brim of his straw hat with a nail tucked into the band, the first one he had driven when he established Lehman Brothers Home Construction. His younger brother Lemuel had removed and replaced it, then gifted it to Jack to remind him that anything big started small.

"Come to see how things are coming along, have you?" Jack went on, not giving them a chance to respond. He talked too much when he was nervous. "Afraid there's nothing to see just yet." He glanced over his shoulder in the direction of where the footing would go in. "A few days from now, when we have the foundation in, you'll be able to get an idea of the size and shape of the place."

"Come to work," Felty declared. He was dressed typically for an Amish man his age except for his lime-green plastic sunglasses, which advertised an insurance company. "Tell me where you want me, *sohn*."

Beth looked at her father and then back at Jack. "*Dat* isn't here to work," she said. "He just walked over with me from the house." She didn't smile at Jack. "I've come to check up on you."

Jack felt his grin sag. She was checking on him? What was that supposed to mean?

And what did Felty mean he'd come to work? Jack wasn't aware that Felty *could* work anymore. That was why the Koffman sisters were so adamant that the store go up quickly. The hard truth was that they needed the income the business would provide.

"Need me to start digging?" Felty asked.

"How long do you think the foundation will take?" Beth asked, talking over her *dat*.

Jack looked from Felty to Beth and decided to tackle the less daunting of the two first. "Well, Felty," he said. "Not much for you to do today. We're just finishing up staking out the foundation. Maybe you ought to see if it looks right to you. I know you're a mason. That's my brother Lemuel." He pointed. "And that's Mark, part of my crew."

Clutching an ancient leather tool bag, Felty squinted at the young men who were working. "That boy wearing a red hat?" he asked.

Jack glanced in their direction, then back at Felty. He hadn't even noticed that his new hire wasn't wearing a straw hat. That would change once the warmer days came. "Mark? *Ya*, he is wearing a red hat. A ball cap. He's Mennonite, so he doesn't have to worry about what a bishop will think. I believe your girls know his sister. Rosie?"

Beth brushed her father's arm with her fingertips. "Rosie Miller. You remember her. You like her," she told him. "She and her brother live near Raber's. Rosie's been to our house, *Dat*. A few weeks ago she brought you ice cream she'd made."

Felty worked his jaw thoughtfully. "Don't remember that." He looked at Beth. "I liked it? The ice cream?"

She grinned at her father. "*Ya*, you had seconds."

He nodded thoughtfully as he walked away, tool bag in hand. "Hope it was chocolate."

For a moment there was a softness to Beth's face that made her more than pretty; it made her beautiful. And then she turned to Jack and the softness was gone. Narrowing her gaze, she planted her hands on her hips. She wore a green dress under her denim barn coat and a navy blue headscarf tied at her nape to cover her hair. "Eleanor has put me in charge of the store," she told him without preamble. "Which means I'm your boss."

"My boss," he said before he had the good sense not to simply repeat what she'd said. "I—"

"Don't like the thought of that much, do you?" she interrupted, taking a step toward him.

Without realizing it, Jack took a step back. Beth had him feeling all off-kilter and he didn't like it much. "Wh—what do you mean?"

"I mean I'm sure you don't like the idea of working for a woman. Having to answer to one." She shrugged. "I understand. Some men are like that." Her tone wasn't complimentary. "In our parents' generation, Amish women stayed in the kitchen and gardens. Men liked it that way. But not anymore, Jack. Nowadays, women take on a bigger part in decisions for the family, and sometimes they make the decisions. So if you don't like it, you should say so now." She glanced in the direction of the worksite. Lemuel and Mark were marking off the measurements with stakes and strings, and

Felty was chatting with them. "I'd be willing to let you out of the agreement," Beth continued. "Return our deposit and that will be the end of it."

"The end of what?" he asked, knitting his brows.

"The contract you and Eleanor signed."

He drew back. She was trying to *cancel* his contract?

He wasn't a man easily angered, but he felt heat flicker deep in his belly and the nape of his neck became warm and prickly. She couldn't cancel his contract!

Could she?

His thoughts raced. If she canceled the job now, his business would go under before it started. And then he would have to admit that his father had been right. His *dat* had said an Amish man couldn't run a construction business without trucks and the other trappings of the English. When Jack had asked to borrow money from his *vadder*, the older man had refused his request, saying it wasn't a good lend. He said there were too many ways for Jack to fail.

Jack felt like he couldn't catch his breath. He'd had several renovation jobs over the last few months and built a porch, but the Koffman store was his first big build. Previously Jack had worked on a construction crew and done side jobs. He'd recently quit his full-time job for a chance to prove to his father that he could run his own business. Jack had borrowed money from his grandfather in Wisconsin, who believed in his grandson's dream. Jack had bought the essential tools he couldn't borrow and a generator to charge the batteries that went into the new tools. Using the same tools of the trade that Englishers had was the only way he, as an Amish man, could compete with them.

Jack struggled not to panic. He couldn't let Beth do this to him. If he lost this job, he wouldn't be able to pay his grandfather's money back by the end of the summer as promised.

Jack swallowed hard and met Beth's gaze. "I don't want out of the contract," he said, trying to sound casual. "I want to build your store. It will be good for your family and the whole community. My mother and sisters have been talking about the convenience of being able to buy everyday items without having to ride all the way to town."

Silent, she stared at him sternly.

Jack wished she wouldn't look at him that

way. It made him feel uncertain of himself. "And…and I don't mind working for women. For you," he went on, because he couldn't stand the tension that hung between them. He shrugged. "I don't mind strong women, in fact…in fact," he repeated, "I like a woman who knows what's what. I have a lot of respect for women," he added, hoping his bravado didn't sound as hollow as it felt.

Beth folded her arms over her chest. "That right?" she asked testily. "Hmm. That's hard to believe. Considering your reputation with women in Honeycomb." She turned away before he could think of a response. "*Dat*, time to go," she called.

"Go where?" Felty asked. "We've got quite a bit of work to do here today. These trenches need to be hand-dug. No other way of doing it."

"*Dat*, you're not digging holes." She waved, beckoning him. "Let's go. We don't want to be in the way and hold things up."

Felty's face fell. "But I don't want to go home. I want to work."

"Beth," Jack said, feeling bad for Felty. He seemed so excited to be there. "He can stay if he wants. I'll keep an eye on him. He'll be fine."

"I am not leaving my father with *you*," Beth snapped. "Best you get to work. I'll see you tomorrow to check on your progression."

Jack watched as she walked to her *dat* and said something Jack couldn't hear, and then he picked up the tool bag. Felty hung his head in disappointment as they walked past Jack on their way back to the house.

His gaze followed them. Was he making a mistake not canceling the contract before he invested any more money in the project? Maybe he could build a house for another customer or drum up some more renovations. Perhaps he could post something on the bulletin board at Byler's store.

But he didn't want to give up the contract. He couldn't. Which meant he'd have to grit his teeth and deal with Beth Koffman and whatever she threw at him.

Jack watched Beth and Felty cross a wide expanse of new grass. As they reached their driveway, his brother's voice startled him.

"Jack?"

Jack glanced up to find Lemuel beside him.

"What was that all about?" Lemuel asked.

"I'm not exactly sure," Jack admitted.

Lem was twenty to Jack's twenty-three, but they looked so alike that folks often got them confused. Lem's blond hair was the color of corn silk, and behind the dark sunglasses, his eyes were the same green as Jack's. He was a good-looking young man, but more importantly, he was a good man. And a good brother, too.

Lemuel chuckled. "I think that's the first woman I've ever seen get the better of you."

Jack pulled a face. "She didn't get the better of me."

"Recht." Lem sounded amused. "Not at Raber's last week either?"

Jack stared at his brother. "How do you know about that?"

"Same way everyone else in Honeycomb knows. Amish telegraph. Lavinia Yoder told someone, who told someone, who told me."

Jack gestured lamely in Beth's direction. "She says she'll oversee the build now, not Eleanor."

"Is she, now?" Lem hesitated and then went on. "You know I always liked Willa. Pretty girl, but she wasn't right for you."

Jack didn't respond.

"But that one," Lem continued, pointing in the direction Beth had gone. "She seems like the kind of woman you need. You'd be wise to ask her out before someone else does."

Jack wondered why everyone wanted to tell him *now* that Willa wasn't a good match for him rather than when he was dating her. Instead, he mumbled, "Time to get back to work." As he strode away, he thought, *Beth Koffman is the last woman on earth I want to date.*

Wednesday morning, Beth walked across Rosie Miller's porch, carrying a basket of giant chocolate chip cookies. As she approached the door, she glanced back. Willa had stopped in the driveway to talk to her friend's brother Mark. Stopping to flirt with him was more like it, Beth observed. Then she smiled, chastising herself. This was a good thing because it meant Willa's heartbreak over Jack was easing.

Beth knocked on the door. As she waited, she heard a country song playing on the radio with Rosie jumping in on the chorus. There were things about Rosie's life that Beth envied, and listening to music on the radio was one of them. Not that she wanted to become Mennonite. She was happy in the life she had been born into as an Old Order Amish woman, and she knew it was her place. That didn't mean she wasn't secretly intrigued by the idea of being able to sing loudly and joyfully a tune that wasn't a hymn.

Beth took another look at her sister. Willa and Mark were still talking, and she wondered why Mark was there and not at work on their store. Had he taken the day off? Returning her attention to the door, she knocked again, hopefully loud enough to be heard.

Suddenly the music got quieter, and Rosie called, "Coming!"

Rosie wasn't expecting her, so Beth hoped the visit wouldn't be inconvenient. She'd almost stopped by the previous day on her way home from Spence's Bazaar to see if it would be okay if she and Willa came today. However, she and Cora had had their father with them and he'd worn himself out looking for bargains in the flea market side of the business.

If Beth had a cell phone, she could have called Rosie, but neither she nor her sisters owned one, and she didn't like to borrow her future brother-in-law's unless it was to make a doctor's appointment or something important. Once the store was built, the sisters had agreed they'd have a landline installed there. They'd already gotten permission from their bishop, who also happened to be their uncle by marriage. The phone would be primarily for the business but could be used for personal reasons.

The door swung open and Rosie greeted Beth with a big smile. She was a pretty woman in her midtwenties with pale blue eyes and skin the color of coffee with milk in it. Rosie had grown up Amish in Indiana, but when she was in her early teens, her parents had left the church and become Mennonite. They had relocated to Delaware to be nearer to her mother's family. Rosie had wed, but the marriage had been brief. Her husband had died, and her brother had moved in with her so she wouldn't be alone.

"I didn't know you were coming today!" Rosie hugged Beth and stepped back to let her in.

"It's okay, though, isn't it?" Beth held up the basket of cookies. "You were talking about trying your hand at making homemade ice cream sandwiches so Willa and I brought some cookies we made. I thought it might be fun to make them together."

"Of course, it's all right if you're here! I've told you a hundred times. Come anytime you like. Come every day. It gets so boring being home alone all the time. Where's Willa?" She gazed outside and then said, "Ah, mystery solved. She's talking to Mark."

"You mean flirting with him." Beth followed her into her bright kitchen. The walls were painted a pretty grass green that complimented the white cabinets well. The windows were graced with white and green gingham curtains, making the room look like it had come out of a magazine.

Rosie and her husband had purchased the manufactured ranch-style home and despite pressure from her parents, she had refused to move back in with them after she lost him. Beth didn't know if she would have been brave enough to stay in a house alone, but she admired her friend's strength and sense of independence. Thankfully it had all worked out, because when Mark started trade school, he'd moved in to keep her company and gain some independence from their parents.

"So what if she's flirting a bit?" Rosie shrugged. She wore an adorable yellow and green dotted print dress, knee socks and clogs, and a lace prayer *kapp* that looked more like a doily than the stiff organza *kapp* Beth wore. "It means she's finally over Jack, doesn't it?"

"How could she?" Beth set the basket of cookies on the kitchen table, where a vase of white tulips rested in the center. "She was in love with him."

Rosie frowned. "Hmm. Do you think she was *really* in love with him?" She shook her head. "I don't think she was. I think she was in love with the *idea* of being in love with him. Peppermint tea?"

Beth always appreciated Rosie's honesty. She wasn't the kind of woman who held anything back. "*Ya*, I'd like some tea. Do you have time to give the ice cream sandwiches a try?" She retrieved three white mugs from a cupboard while Rosie put on the electric teakettle.

"I have nothing but free time. That'll be fun. I'm so glad you came," Rosie told her. "I wasn't sure how I was going to spend my day. My house is clean, the laundry is done and I can't possibly straighten out my closet again. I get bored at home these days," she continued as she measured out loose tea leaves into a flowered teapot. "I wonder if I shouldn't get a job. Though if I do, Mark says I'll have to work on my driving, because with him working fulltime for Jack Lehman now, he can't always be available to take me where I need to go."

"Maybe you'd like to work for us once the store is built," Beth suggested. "Speaking of the store, isn't Mark supposed to be at our place working today?" She realized now that she hadn't seen his truck when she and Willa had left their house. She felt a flicker of annoyance, thinking that if Jack didn't hire a big enough crew, how would he get the store built in the time he had promised?

"Oh, he's working today. He was on the job before seven this morning. He just forgot the lunch I'd packed for him. He ran into Dover to get some supplies, and then he swung by to pick up his lunch sack. Mark says things are moving right along. He thinks the foundation will be done by tomorrow."

"News to me. When I checked in with Jack yesterday, he said he didn't know when it would be finished."

"I don't know anything about construction. I don't know if it takes two days or two weeks to lay a foundation. But I do know Jack has been good to Mark. He pays him well and has offered to teach Mark the building trade." The kettle clicked off and Rosie poured hot water over the tea leaves in the teapot. "I have to admit I wasn't thrilled at first with the idea of Mark working for him."

"Because of Willa?"

"Sort of." Rosie leaned against the counter, crossing her arms over her chest. "I'm not sure he's the kind of man I want influencing my little brother." She met Beth's gaze. "He doesn't have a good reputation at Honeycomb Mennonite Church among parents, if you know what I mean. There are rumors."

"What kind of rumors?"

"It's not only Willa who's had trouble with him," Rosie said. "He's got a reputation for being a player."

"A *player*?" Beth asked.

"You know. A playboy?" Rosie arched her eyebrows. "A man about town. I've heard mothers talk about him and not in a positive light. The single girls all think he's handsome but they've been warned to stay away from him."

Beth didn't quite know what it meant to be a player or a playboy, but she could read between the lines well enough to know neither her sister nor any other girl in Honeycomb ought to be walking out with him. "Has he dated Mennonite girls?" she asked, unsure if she was horrified or fascinated. Amish men left the church sometimes and when they did, they often became Mennonite, but to her knowledge, only two men had left their community in the last ten years.

"I don't think so but I don't know any details." Rosie carried the teapot to the table. "I mean, I appreciate that Jack is giving Mark a chance to work in construction now that he's done with school. I hope he doesn't take a page from Jack's book on how to treat women. Otherwise—" she pulled out a chair to sit down "—he'll be in big trouble with me."

Beth smiled with satisfaction as she took a chair at the table. Rosie's information only strengthened her belief that Jack breaking up with Willa was a blessing in disguise.

Chapter Four

Sunday afternoon, Beth slipped into Edna Mast's pantry with a dessert plate of Jello ribbon salad. After the long church service and hubbub of serving and cleanup following the midday meal, she needed a moment to herself. She loved her large, close-knit church community, but sometimes she needed time alone with her thoughts. This was particularly true after the week she'd had.

She had discovered that Jack Lehman was a complicated man. Previously, she'd only known him through Willa. Having attributed certain characteristics to him based on her sister's opinion and Rosie's, she struggled to come to terms with the bright, energetic, hardworking man, who never grew impatient with her many questions. In fact, he seemed to enjoy talking about his work with her. Jack had told her repeatedly that he had no intention of canceling their contract and seemed nonplussed by her visits to check on his progress. In fact, he seemed happy to see her. And the man knew how to turn on the charm to the point that she struggled to resist him. He'd broken her sister's heart, and Beth knew she must keep their relationship strictly business.

Perching on a stool, Beth took a bite of the cool and creamy Jell-O salad. She would ask Edna for her recipe. If Beth substituted sugarfree Jell-O, it would be sweet enough to satisfy her father without raising his blood sugar too much.

As she enjoyed the treat, Beth listened to women laughing and talking as they tidied Edna's kitchen. The eleven families currently in their church district took turns hosting the services held every other Sunday. Edna and her husband, Jim, had a large commercial orchard and used one of their outbuildings for church services. Beth looked forward to whenever the Masts hosted. No matter the time of year, she could smell the mouthwatering aroma of apples and pears and sometimes peaches while she listened to the word of God.

Beth ate another forkful of Jell-O salad with

a sigh as her thoughts drifted back to her week. Jack had completed the concrete block foundation and was supposed to begin framing up the building the next morning. Four out of the five days, she'd checked on the progress, but she'd had difficulty escaping from her father to the site without him knowing. When she'd mentioned to Jack that she'd snuck out the front door so her father wouldn't see her go, Jack again had offered to let him "hang out" with his work crew. That had annoyed her. What did Jack know about caring for a parent with dementia?

Beth heard a baby fussing and wondered whose it was. She realized it was a girl she had been friends with in school, Lizzy, who had married the previous year and recently had her first baby. When Lizzy had shown off her little boy that morning, Beth had been surprised by how eager she had been to hold him. Beth had never thought much about babies. She hoped to marry someday and, God willing, have children, but she didn't long for an infant like many single women her age did. She'd always assumed that desire would come when she met the right man, the man God intended to be her husband. Why she'd felt an odd yearning this morning when she held little Ezra, she didn't know.

"Beth?" came Jane's voice from the kitchen, her voice pitched higher than usual. "Has anyone seen Beth?"

The concern in her little sister's tone made Beth jump off the stool. Jane and Henry had been outside playing volleyball with a group of girls. Beth hoped no one had been injured. "Here!" she called from the pantry doorway. She dropped the paper plate and plastic fork into a trash can. "What's wrong?"

Jane hurried toward her. "We can't find *Dat.*"

Beth frowned. "What do you mean you can't find him? Who was watching him?"

"Me," Jane said, her voice quivering. "He was sitting on the porch, happy as could be. I could keep my eye on him from where we were playing volleyball. One minute he was there, then the next he was gone."

"Did you check with the other men?" Edna asked from the other side of the kitchen. "I think Jim said they were heading to have a look at the new peach trees we planted."

Jane shook her head. "I did, and he's not with them."

"In the barn?" Lizzy's mother suggested.

"*Ne*, he's not there either."

"How about in your buggy?" Millie's friend Annie asked. "My grandpa used to wait in our buggy when he was ready to go home. Didn't matter if we weren't leaving for hours."

"You check upstairs?" Minnie Koblenz, a woman their mother's age, offered. "When we hosted two weeks ago, I found your *Dat* sound asleep on our bed."

Jane pressed her hand to her forward. "What do we do?" she asked Beth.

"We stay calm," Beth said. "He's here somewhere."

"Don't worry," one of the other women said. "No one here would let him get hurt. Beth's right. He's here. You just haven't found him yet."

"Why don't you start by looking upstairs," Beth suggested to her sister. "As long as Edna doesn't mind." She looked to their hostess.

"Of course not," Edna responded. "I spent two days straightening upstairs. Someone may as well see it."

"You look upstairs," Beth told Jane. "I'll go outside. He likes the apple sorter. Maybe he's there."

"Do you want us to help look?" Edna asked.

Several of the other women chimed in that they'd be happy to join the search for Felty.

"*Ne*, not yet. I don't want to upset him. I'm sure he's around here somewhere. We'll find him." Beth met Jane's gaze again and spoke softly. "Go through all the rooms upstairs. I'll head outside to look for him. When I run into one of our sisters, *other than Eleanor*, I'll let them know we're looking for *Dat*."

"You don't think we should tell Ellie?" Jane whispered.

Beth smiled and whispered back. "Not if we don't have to. I saw her talking to Edna's son Jon. *Alone*."

Jane's eyes widened as she pressed her lips together as if she was trying not to smile. Her sister Eleanor had it in her head that no man would ever want to marry her because she'd had her foot amputated. It didn't matter how often Beth and her sisters argued with Eleanor or how they tried to prove her wrong. Eleanor was certain she would be an old maid until the day she died. The fact that her sister was chatting with Jon Mast, a handsome man the same age as Ellie, was encouraging.

Beth reached out and squeezed Jane's shoulder. "Go. We'll find him. Try not to worry."

Jane hurried out of the kitchen toward the

hall, and Beth headed in the opposite direction and the back door.

"You certain you don't want help?" Edna called after her.

"Ne." Beth gave a wave over her head as she entered the mudroom. "We'll find him."

Outside, Beth stepped onto the covered porch and down the stairs, her gaze sweeping across the side yard in the direction of the orchard. As she looked for her father, she smiled.

The previous autumn, Millie's romance with Elden had begun right here at a benefit auction when he'd purchased an apple galette she'd baked. Beth wasn't the jealous type, but sometimes she couldn't help but wonder if anyone would ever pursue her the way Elden had Millie. Would any man ever love her the way Elden loved her sister?

Beth sighed, her thoughts returning to the problem at hand. She couldn't find her father anywhere. Should she look for him in the orchard? Maybe he'd gone for a walk there. Earlier he'd told Millie about the honeybees pollinating the fruit trees. Maybe he'd gone into the orchard for a closer look.

A red rubber ball like the kind Millie had played kickball with as a schoolgirl shot past her, and she heard a little boy's laughter, followed by a deeper tone.

Jack appeared near the corner of the house. "I'll get it!" he called.

One of Edna's boys, ten-year-old Alan, ran after Jack.

Jack reached the ball that had rolled to a stop, and as he was about to kick it to the little boy, he caught sight of her. "Beth."

She nodded in greeting.

His brow furrowed beneath his wide-brimmed black Sunday hat. "You *oll recht*?"

"*Ya*, fine," she answered, hoping he would go back to playing ball.

But he didn't. Instead, he walked toward her. "You certain? You look worried."

Beth sighed again and cut her eyes at him. "I'm looking for my *dat*. I don't suppose you've seen him?"

"I haven't," Jack answered, thinking before he spoke. "Not since dinner. He was sitting at the end of my table talking to your uncle, the bishop."

Jack was dressed for Sunday services like all the other men: black pants, a white shirt and a black vest. But somehow he looked different. His clothing was well fitted to his frame and he carried himself better than a lot of men his age.

Beth glanced toward the orchard. "He's got to be around here somewhere," she said.

"Want to play some more?" Alan asked Jack. He was pushing the red ball around with the toe of his Sunday black shoes.

"Not right now. I'm going to help Beth look for Felty."

"I don't need help," Beth insisted.

"Maybe later?" Alan asked Jack.

Jack smiled and tousled the boy's hair. "Maybe later."

Alan nodded, his disappointment was plain on his face. Then he piped up, "I saw Felty."

Beth approached the boy. "When did you see him? Where?"

"A few minutes ago." Alan pointed, and Beth followed his line of vision, then frowned in confusion. "In the house?" she asked.

"The *lane*," Alan answered, waving his hand high as if she could see through the house or over the roof. "Felty was walking down the lane."

Beth felt her heart flutter in her chest. "He was leaving?"

Alan shrugged and walked away, kicking the ball.

Beth took off, walking briskly around the side of the house.

Jack fell in beside her. "I'll help you look."

"No need." They rounded the house and she cut across the grass toward the long gravel driveway.

"I'd say there *is* a need."

Beth glanced at him, making no attempt to hide her displeasure.

He met her gaze and exhaled in exasperation. "Look, Beth. You don't like me. That's pretty clear. As to why, we won't get into it right now. I don't know what Willa told you, but there's are always two sides—"

"What she told me was that you were two-timing her," Beth interrupted angrily, shaking a finger at him. "You were walking out with her and Barbara Troyer at the same time. And Barbara even admitted she was dating you."

"There are always two sides to every story," Jack said firmly. "So when you're ready to hear my side, let me know." He was walking fast enough that she had to take a double stride every few steps to keep with him. "But this isn't the time or the place, Beth. Right now we need to find your *vadder*."

Beth nodded, feeling embarrassed as a lump of emotion rose in her throat. Suddenly she fought tears. "Where could he have gone?" she asked as they reached where the lane met the blacktop county road.

"If he went this way, my guess is that he intended to go home."

Beth took a shuddering breath. "But it's three miles." The two turned in the direction of the Koffman farm in silent agreement.

"I'm sure he's fine," Jack said.

She sniffed, patting her dress for a handkerchief. "I don't know if he even knows the way home. He's gotten so forgetful." Still looking for her handkerchief, she remembered she'd left it home. Just before leaving for church that morning she'd been headed back to her bedroom to fetch one, but her father had been standing in the hall trying to pull on his suspenders and she'd stopped to help him. After that, she must have forgotten about bringing one.

"*Gott* will keep him safe," Jack said quietly. "Here." He pushed a neatly pressed white handkerchief into her hand. "Don't worry. It's clean."

Beth didn't know what overcame her. She was in by no means a jovial mood, but she laughed at his comment. Men were such strange creatures.

Ten minutes later and half a mile down the road, Beth and Jack found her father sitting on a fallen log near the edge of a woods owned by Englishers. Jim Mast's big black Labrador retriever sat beside him, its ears perked as if on guard.

"*Dat*!" Beth cried. She grasped the skirt of her black Sunday dress to keep from tripping and rushed toward him. Without thought, she leaped the small drainage ditch between them and ran through the grass. "Are you all right?" she cried. "Are you hurt?"

Her father looked up at her, his face blank. She stared into his eyes the same color as her own for a moment. At last, he exhaled her name, "Beth," as if he had just realized who she was.

Tears sprang in her eyes out of relief that she had found him and from sadness for the state of his mind. And he had been so sharp-minded that morning. He had seemed like the man she had known all her life, trying to hustle his girls out of the house to make it to church on time.

"*Dat*, what are you doing here?" Beth asked gently. "You gave us a fright. We couldn't find you at Jim and Edna's."

"Time to go home," he answered. "I was

ready to go home. Got a herd of cows to milk. Chickens to feed."

Beth pressed her lips together. There was no herd of dairy cows anymore. There hadn't been in at least ten years. Now they just had two cows, which Henry milked most days.

Jack stood beside her. "Hey, Felty. Who's your friend?" He pointed at the Labrador.

Her father stroked the Lab's sleek, shiny coat. "He's my dog. I don't recollect his name at the moment, but that's *oll recht*." He patted the animal affectionately.

Beth looked at Jack, who stood there as if he walked the roads searching for lost fathers every day. She returned her attention to her *dat*. "We should head home." She pointed down the road. "Jack can let Ellie know we walked home."

Her father shook his head. Stroked the dog. "Too tired to walk the rest of the way. It's gotten farther, I think." Then he smirked. "Of course, it's not farther. I just got older."

Beth reached out to him with both hands. 'Let's get you to your feet. It's not *that* far home. We can walk it together. We'll go slow. Or…or we could walk back to Jim and Edna's and get the buggy."

He shook his head. "*Ne.* I'm tired of walking. We'll sit here, the dog and me."

"*Dat*—" The feel of Jack's hand on her shoulder startled her, and Beth locked gazes with him.

Jack tilted his head slightly, indicating he wanted to speak with her privately. She glanced at her *dat,* and seeing the stubborn look on his face, she moved a few feet away with Jack following.

"Look," Jack said quietly. "He looks tired. Maybe trying to walk him home or back to the Masts' might not be the best idea."

Beth's temper flared. "Who do you think you are, telling me what's best for my father?" she demanded. But as soon as the words came out of her mouth, she regretted them.

Because Jack was right. As much as she hated to admit it, he was right and she was wrong. Embarrassed, she pressed her hand to her forehead. Though it was late afternoon, the sun was unseasonably warm and her black Sunday dress and white apron were hot. She gazed up at the clouds, then at her father and the dog, debating what to do.

Jack remained silent and then said, "How about I go back to the Masts', let your sisters know your *vadder* is fine and grab our wagon.

Then I'll come back for you both. You can sit here with your *dat*. I'll be right back to take you home."

Beth narrowed her eyes as she studied his handsome face. Nothing made sense in her mind with Jack. Willa and Rosie had said things about him that didn't mesh with the kind man standing before her calmly discussing a plan to get her father home while she tried not to dissolve into tears.

"Why would you do that?" she asked.

He frowned, tilting his head. "Why wouldn't I? I've known your father since I was on lead strings. Felty is a member of my church, of the Honeycomb community." He hesitated. "Wouldn't you do the same thing for me if my *dat* was sitting on that log right now?"

She lowered her gaze to stare at her black leather shoes. "Of course, I would, but…" *But what?* What did she want to say? *But you're a player?* But players don't do nice things like this for other people.

The thought seemed absurd. She didn't even really understand what a *player* was. Or precisely what Rosie had meant by it.

Her mother had always taught her to reach her own conclusions, especially when it came to a person's character. *People are compli-*

cated, she used to say. Beth thought she knew who Jack was, but *that* man wasn't the man standing in front of her.

Beth inhaled a deep breath, glanced at her father and, seeing that he hadn't moved, she looked at Jack. "If you would do that for us, I'd appreciate it."

"*Goot*, so it's a plan. You wait right here," he told her. "I'll be back before you've had time to get comfortable on that log. It's going to be all right, Beth. Your *dat's* going to be fine." He smiled, but it wasn't the big, handsome smile she'd seen him flash at other women. It was a kind smile that made her feel like everything would be all right.

She pressed her lips together and nodded. Then she watched him cross the ditch. When he reached the paved road, she called after him, "What about the dog?"

Jack turned and shrugged. "He can ride with us and I'll bring him home after I drop you off. I'm going to have to come back for my brothers anyway. Not enough room in the family buggy."

Then he smiled and, against all reason, Beth found herself smiling back at him.

Jack eased the wagon into the Koffman's barnyard less than an hour later. They had barely rolled to a stop when Felty clambered down before he or Beth could assist him.

"Come on, dog," Felty said, landing easily on his feet. "Let's go, boy." He tapped his leg. "We've got cows to milk."

The black Labrador didn't move.

"Come on. What are you waiting for?" Felty asked the dog.

The Masts' pup looked down at him but still didn't move.

"*Dat*, he can't stay here," Beth said from the wagon seat beside Jack. "He's not our dog."

Felty stared at the Labrador for a long moment. "He's not?"

"*Ne*," she said. "We don't have a dog."

Felty chewed that over in his mind before he shrugged and said, "I knew that." He turned and walked away, throwing his hand up in farewell as he headed for the back porch. "See you bright and early tomorrow, Jack! Time to get to the business of framing up."

"Not a lot for you to do tomorrow, Felty," Jack said. "I plan to spend the whole day getting ready to frame. You know, snapping lines, cutting jack studs and building headers. The exterior walls should start going up Tuesday."

"Tuesday," Felty repeated as he walked.

When Felty walked up the porch steps, Jack

glanced at Beth next to him, pleasantly surprised that she was still sitting beside him. She sat with her hands in her lap. Lost in her thoughts, she didn't realize he was watching her. He noticed her cheeks were a rosy color, and a lock of hair had slipped from her white prayer *kapp* to curl at her temple. Staring at the reddish-blond tendril, he had a foolish urge to reach out and touch it. He was likely to get a walloping or a tongue-lashing from her if he dared. But there was something about this quiet, thoughtful Beth that intrigued as much as the fiery woman he knew her to be.

He tried to think of something to say, but he sat there silently beside her instead and listened to the call of a mockingbird from a pink dogwood tree that had begun to bloom. The yard was as neat as anyone's in their community, and he marveled at how well the Koffman women were managing without their mother and with their father's illness.

"I'm afraid he's getting worse," Beth said softly.

"You think so?" Jack asked, glancing at her again. "When we talked about the framing, everything he said was spot-on. He knows how to construct a header better than some of my crew."

She turned her head to look at him. "But he thinks he's *part* of your crew."

Jack pressed his lips together. He didn't fancy a walloping from a pretty girl like Beth, but he couldn't hold his tongue. "Maybe he should be."

"Maybe he should be *what*?" she asked, her captivating eyes creasing at the corners.

"Be on my crew."

She rolled her eyes at him, her tone curt when she spoke. "Jack, you know very well—"

"Beth," he interrupted. "Just calm down a minute and—"

"I *am* calm," she insisted. "Very calm."

He paused a moment, waiting for her to become calm again and then went on. "He really wants to help build your store."

"How can he work construction? He believes that dog is his."

"Maybe his hands will remember what to do."

She nibbled on her lower lip. "Eleanor would never agree to it."

She was saying no, but her tone suggested she might be considering his proposal. "Beth," he said, "just because a man suffers from memory loss doesn't mean he doesn't want to take care of his family. It doesn't mean he doesn't want to feel useful."

She was quiet for a moment. "I hadn't thought about that." Her lashes fluttered and she lifted her gaze to meet his. "It's so hard to see him like this. I feel like we're losing him, too," she murmured, her words catching in her throat.

The sound of the pain in her voice caught him off guard, and he glanced away, surprised by the feelings she stirred inside him. Hearing her heartbreak, he wanted to cover her hand with his. He wanted to tell her that everything would be all right, that *Gott* was with her and her father. But he wasn't used to talking that way to girls. It wasn't what they wanted from him. What they wanted, he had learned years ago was flirtation and fun. It was almost as if because of the way he looked, girls assumed that was all he was good for.

Beth climbed down from the wagon and he watched her, hating to see her go. "Planning to check up on me tomorrow?"

"It's our store you're building," she retorted. "I have a right to check on how it's going. We're paying you a lot of money to build it."

"I'm not saying you shouldn't keep track of how it's going. You're welcome on the job site any time." He shrugged. "I just wondered if you'd be by."

Beth looked up at him. "Maybe I will, maybe I won't. Sounds like you won't have much to show for the day you have planned for tomorrow."

He rubbed the smooth leather of the reins between his fingers. "It's like that in construction. Days you spent preparing, planning, you don't see much getting done. But the boss of the crew I used to work on taught me how important the planning stages are. It all goes faster and better when you're well prepared. If all goes well, I think we'll have the outer walls done by Friday. The second story will take longer than the first."

"But it's only half the size of the downstairs, and you're leaving it unfinished." She crossed her arms, annoyance in her voice. "You were the one who suggested we only do a story and a half. You said it would be cheaper and go together faster."

"*Ya*, but you want it done right, don't you?" He went on without waiting for her to respond. "I know you do. And I do, too. So have some faith in me." He smiled at her.

She held his gaze for a long moment and then turned away and started toward the house. Halfway up the walk, she halted to look back at him. "Thank you again, Jack," she said, her tone utterly different from a moment ago. "For helping me find *Dat* and bringing us home. I don't know what I would done if it hadn't been for you"

"*Gern gschehne.*" He watched her enter the house and then eased the wagon back down her lane, thinking that might have been the sweetest thank-you he'd ever heard.

Chapter Five

Beth felt a strange sense of excitement Tuesday morning as she dressed, shared breakfast with her family and helped tidy up. She told herself she was eager to get to the building site to see the framing go up. She didn't dare admit that she looked forward to seeing Jack.

The previous day she hadn't gone to the worksite. She told herself she had better things to do than to watch him snap chalk lines, but the truth was that she saw him in a different light than she had before and that scared her. On Sunday the two-timing cheat had been kind to her and her father. He had gone out of his way to help her and had acted as if his efforts to find her father and then see him home safely were nothing. And after Jack had collected her and her father and the dog, he had chatted with her all the way home as if they had been friends their whole lives. They had talked about the church service and the preacher's message, and he had impressed her with his insight into the scripture. Then he switched topics and asked her opinion on possibly adding a second window to the store's original plan. He thought hanging double windows rather than the single on the south side would give additional natural light to the back room where employees would take breaks.

As they had turned into her driveway, Beth wished the ride had been longer. She'd enjoyed her conversation with Jack too much to want it to end. She liked that he'd asked her thoughts on both the sermon and the window, making her wonder about the man sitting next to her. Could he be the same Jack Lehman both Willa and Rosie had said terrible things about?

Beth thought herself to be a good judge of character, and something about Jack didn't make sense. The man she'd ridden home with didn't seem like the kind who could do what he had done to Willa. But then facts were the facts, weren't they? That's what she kept telling herself. She needed to keep Willa in mind when Jack started flashing that handsome smile at her.

As Beth wiped the table of muffin crumbs left behind by her father, she noticed Jane whispering to Cora in the corner of the kitchen. Jane said something Beth couldn't hear, and then Cora shook her head vehemently, stealing glances at her other sisters.

Watching them, Beth pushed crumbs into her hand with a dishrag. "*Oll recht*," she said. "What's going on with you two?"

Both girls fell silent as they looked at Beth and then each other again.

"Tell them," Jane told Cora, her eyes wide with exasperation.

Beth carried the crumbs to the trash can. "Tell us what?"

"Cora's got a secret," Willa sang as she slid a pitcher of fresh milk into the refrigerator. "It's Andy Yoder, isn't it? Andy Yoder asked if he could bring you home from the singing next weekend, didn't he?" She clapped her hands together. "I knew it! I saw him talking to you when you were playing volleyball Sunday."

Cora frowned, pushing her wireframe glasses farther up on her nose. "Andy was *not* asking me if I'd ride home with him."

Willa walked toward her, waggling her finger. "No fibbing. We're going to find out eventually." She smiled mischievously. "Andy is so handsome. And such a nice boy. He—"

"*Oll recht!* Fine, if you must know," Cora interrupted, obviously perturbed with all of them, "Andy wasn't asking if he could drive me home, *Willa.*" She exhaled loudly. "He asked me if I thought *you* would ride home with him after the singing."

Jane's eyes widened and she pressed her hand to her cheek. "*Ne!* He didn't," she said with obvious delight.

Cora crossed her arms, unmoved by her sister's pleasure. Cora wasn't jealous of Willa's popularity with the boys, but she sometimes expressed her confusion about what Willa possessed that attracted men to her like bees to flowers. Cora, who was a year older than Willa, saw Willa's popularity as a reflection of how *unpopular* she was.

Willa giggled behind her hand. "Oh, I don't know if I'm ready for that yet. Not after Jack, but—"she laughed again "—that's so sweet of Andy." She pressed her lips together. "I should consider it, shouldn't I? It would be rude if I didn't."

Jane rolled her eyes. "Willa, not everything is about you." She looked at Cora. "Tell them," she insisted. "Or I will."

"What's going on?" Eleanor asked. She passed a stack of dried plates to Millie to put them away. "No secrets," she reminded Cora as she turned to the dirty dishes still in the sink. "We're not a family with secrets."

Cora shot their little sister an annoyed look and exhaled sharply, making it clear that she wasn't being forthright voluntarily. "Amos Lehman spoke privately to me Sunday. The school board asked him to."

Eleanor swung around, giving Cora her full attention. "Whatever about?"

Cora crossed the kitchen toward her. "Don't say no yet," she said tersely. "Don't tell me no before you've heard what I have to say. What the school board has to say."

Eleanor gave her a look that they had all seen on their mother's face when she was about to lose her patience. "I'm listening."

Jane took a step back, meeting Beth's gaze across the room. Jane's face had an *oh no* expression on it; she must have been thinking the same thing Beth was thinking. Here we go again. Cora and Eleanor had been butting heads over various stuff for the last few months. Cora seemed mild-mannered to most but had a temper that all of them tried to avoid riling up whenever possible. She was stubborn, too, and didn't give in easily. In spite of being so small, she was feisty.

"Amos says the school board wants me to apply for a new schoolteacher position that will be coming up in the fall," Cora blurted.

Eleanor cut her eyes at Cora. "Absolutely not."

"See," Cora told Jane, gesturing with a hand toward Eleanor. "This is why I didn't want to say anything. Not yet. Because I don't have any of the details. All I know right now is that there will be a vacant position. Amos said the school board wants me to come to a meeting and hear about their plans."

Eleanor started to say something, but Cora kept talking.

"Ellie, I know you don't want us working away from the house, but think about it. If I were teaching, I would have a monthly salary. It would be a bit of a cushion we could live on until the store starts making a profit. And..." She balled her small hands into fists. "And I really want this job. You know I've always dreamed of being a schoolteacher. And if *Mam* hadn't died—" Cora's voice caught in her throat. She didn't finish what she was going to say, but she didn't have to.

Beth and her sisters knew precisely what

Cora was thinking. *Had their mother not died, she would not only have allowed Cora to apply for the job but would have encouraged her to do so.*

Everyone in the kitchen stood perfectly still for a moment. No one spoke.

Then Eleanor said, "I thought the new school was being built near Elden's uncle's place. That's miles from here. Too far to walk. You'd have to take the buggy every day and that would leave us without it."

"Amos said the school board doesn't know which school they'll be hiring for," Cora gushed. "They may build a new school or add on to one of the other schools. Enrollments are up at some schools, down at others. When the Joe Yoders moved to Kentucky in January, they took nine children out of the Peach Blossom School."

Eleanor looked as if she was about to say something when the back door flew open with a bang, and a gust of spring air blew into the kitchen.

"Is *Dat* in here?" Henry called, her tone filled with frustration.

"*Nay.*" Eleanor replied. "I thought he was with *you.*"

Henry hovered in the doorway between the

kitchen and the mudroom. She wore knee-high rubber boots and a dirty barn coat. On her head was one of their father's knit caps."

"He *was* with me. He wanted to help me set the new nesting boxes for the chicken." She threw up her hands in exasperation. "I went to the toolshed to get a hammer for him and he was gone when I got back."

Eleanor closed her eyes for a moment. When she opened them, she held up her finger to Cora. "We'll discuss this later."

"Does that mean you'll consider the idea?" Cora asked hopefully.

"It means we'll discuss it later." She turned to Henry. "You sure he's not in the barn? Maybe looking for the new kittens? I think Snowball keeps moving them because he won't leave them alone. Yesterday I found one in his coat pocket. Snowball was beside herself."

"If he's in the barnyard, I can't find him. And he doesn't answer when I call him."

It only took Beth a moment to figure out where their father was and she strode toward the mudroom. "It's okay." She rubbed Eleanor's back as she walked past her. "I know where he is. I'll fetch him."

Beth grabbed her coat and hurried out the back door. She was halfway down the driveway when she spotted Rosie's brother Mark walking toward her. They met halfway.

"My *dat*," she said with exasperation.

"Safe and sound. Jack asked me to come up to the house and let you know he's with us."

"Thank you." She fell into step beside him and they headed toward the store. "He was with Henry. She only left him for a few minutes, but he managed to get away." She gave a little laugh. She honestly hadn't been worried about him because she knew well that he'd gone to the building site, but she still felt a sense of relief.

She and Mark walked together toward the store talking about the weather. She found her father seated on the tailgate of his truck beside Jack, and she thanked Mark again as he returned to his work.

"*Dat*," Beth said, stopping in front of him. She rested her hands on her hips. "Henry's been looking for you."

Without responding, her father slurped from a cup that had come from the thermos between him and Jack.

She caught the scent of fresh, hot coffee in the cool morning air and rolled her eyes. "Are you drinking someone else's coffee?" She looked at Jack. "I'm so sorry."

Jack shrugged and smiled. "It's fine. It's a big thermos."

She sighed. "Thank you for sending Mark. I guessed where he was as soon as Henry told us he was missing, but he gave Henry a scare."

"Well," her father declared to no one in particular. "Guess I best get back to work. These walls aren't going to build themselves." He jumped down from the tailgate, slurped the last of the coffee, screwed the cap back on Jack's thermos and walked away.

Beth watched him go and then looked at Jack, still seated on the tailgate.

"Sit down for a sec." He patted the space beside him.

She hesitated. Jack was looking awfully handsome this morning in a pair of dark sunglasses. *Too handsome.* "I'd planned on coming down here anyway. I was hoping to watch the first wall put in place," she said, directing her attention to the new foundation.

"Then you're just in time. Mark and Lem and Peter were finishing up when your dad showed for work."

She eyed him with disapproval. "My *dat* is not here to work, Jack. That's not going to happen."

"Come on, Beth." Jack hopped down from

the bed of the white truck. "Let him help." He held up his hand. "Just for a few hours." He shrugged. "Then I'll walk him back to the house. Or you could come back for him and see how what we've gotten done."

"I don't know how much work you'd get done while keeping an eye on him," she said crossly. "He can be a handful. You never know when he'll decide to follow a rabbit or walk to Byler's to get an ice cream cone."

"I'm not worried about that." Jack pulled off his sunglasses to meet her gaze. "I reckon he'd stay right here with us."

She eyed him suspiciously, trying to figure out why he was so set on her *dat* being here. Did he really want him or did he have some ulterior motive? "Why would you want to take responsibility for him? He's not your *dat*."

"Because he wants to be here." His grin was lazy. "And because I like you, Beth. I like doing something nice for a pretty girl like yourself."

Beth's mouth went dry and she stared at him for a moment, his comment taking her completely off guard.

Was he *flirting* with her?

She quickly looked away. She prided herself in being a person who always knew what to do and say in any situation, but not this time. Men as good-looking and confident as Jack didn't flirt with women like her. They flirted with the Willas of the world. He couldn't possibly be interested in her.

Could he?

Thankfully, she didn't have to say a word because he kept talking. "It's a beautiful day. I think we'll get the whole first floor framed up before we quit for the day. I bet Felty would like to see the walls go up."

She glanced in her father's direction and watched as he picked up a two-by-four from a pile of fresh lumber and carried it toward the other men. Then she looked back at Jack. "I am not leaving my father here. I'm paying you to put up the building, not keep track of my *dat*."

He shrugged. "Suit yourself." He walked away, motioning for her to go with him. "It looks like they're ready to raise that first wall. Watch us, and then I'll show you where I think those double windows ought to go. I also have a question about one of the interior walls."

She took two quick steps to catch up with Jack, relieved the flirtation had passed. Yet a tiny part of her wished she had flirted back.

Wished she was the kind of girl who *could* flirt. The type that a man like Jack Lehman wanted to walk out with.

It was going on ten o'clock when Jack wearily hung his hat and jacket in his family's laundry room where he lived with his parents and five siblings who ranged in age from twenty-two down to ten. He had an older brother and sister who were married and lived with their own families, his brother here in Honeycomb and his sister nearby in Seven Poplars.

Most of the windows were dark as he pulled into the barnyard. His parents were early-to-bed, early-to-rise folks, so the whole family was usually in bed by nine thirty. Lem, whom Mark dropped off hours ago, had said he would eat the minute he got home, wash up and go to sleep. Jack intended to do the same. Maybe he'd skip supper, though it had been nine hours since he last ate and his stomach was grumbling.

It had been a long, hard, frustrating day that made him wonder if it had been a mistake to go into the contracting business independently. Nothing had gone right and a lot had gone wrong. Because of two days of torrential rain, he had already been behind schedule, then the lumber delivery that should have arrived two days earlier hadn't come until three in the afternoon. Jack realized that half of the order was missing only after the driver left. Then after tracking down the rest of his order, he'd discovered that his new employee, Peter, hadn't known that every exterior wall needed a double top plate. The entire wall the crew had constructed needed to be rebuilt.

It was one thing after another, all day long. The only good thing was that Beth hadn't shown up to see how little they'd accomplished because she'd taken her father to see his doctor and get blood work. That she'd been too busy to check on him had been a true blessing from God, because with everything else going on, he wasn't sure how well he could have dealt with her.

It was probably his fault that Lem and the other men had made a mistake on the wall. If Jack had been thinking more about the job at hand and less about his pretty boss, maybe he would have caught the error sooner. The woman had him perplexed beyond understanding. He honestly couldn't tell if she liked or disliked him, which made him appreciate her more.

Jack sighed and headed toward the kitchen.

Should he make himself a sandwich or go to bed hungry? When he opened the door to the kitchen, he was surprised to find that someone had left a battery lantern on the kitchen table that easily sat twelve, and he was startled to see his mother and father still awake and seated at the table.

His mother was darning a sock, his father reading a farming magazine. His mother smiled at the sight of him. "*Guder owed, sohn.* I was beginning to worry about you."

Before Jack could respond to his mother, his father, without looking up from his magazine, said gruffly, "Late to be coming in."

His mother lowered her gaze to her darning.

With an audible sigh, Jack dragged his hand over his face. He wasn't in the mood to talk with his father. To be talked *at* by his father. Jack loved the man, but their relationship was a difficult one. It had been since he reached adulthood, which he found interesting because his *dat* had been such a good father to his children when they were young.

Nowadays, they never understood each other and constantly butted heads. Maybe because once Jack was grown, the chasm became obvious whenever he voiced his opinions. The most significant disagreement between them was that Jack didn't want the same life his father had, unlike his older brother. He didn't want to farm like his father and his grandfather. Wanting to find his own way in the world, he had chosen to work in construction. Owning his own construction business.

"Long day," Jack said. "Everything that could go wrong did, and then some."

"So Lemuel said when he got home at a decent time." His father closed his magazine and got up from his chair. "Don't say I didn't warn you. Not too late to come to your senses and cancel that contract with the Koffmans." He slid his chair in under the table and it squeaked against the hardwood floor. "I don't know what would make you think you should work for Eleanor Koffman. Building a store," he scoffed. "That woman's got as much chance of being able to run a store as you do of building houses for a living." He shook his head. "Not natural for a man to be working for a woman. She ought to be married. Those girls need a man in that house."

There were so many things wrong with what his father had said that Jack didn't know where to start. But he didn't have the energy to argue. Nothing would come of it anyway. His father believed in the old ways. He thought women belonged in the home, raising children and being submissive to their husbands. He didn't see or understand the world his children were facing as adults. Sharar Lehman wouldn't admit that the old way of an Amish man supporting a large family by growing corn and selling vegetables at a roadside stand was no longer viable. He didn't appreciate that some things had to change for their way of life to continue as it had for the two hundred plus years since their ancestors had fled to America searching for religious freedom.

Jack believed that the young men in their community had to join the workforce to provide for their families. And if they must work away from their farms, why not work for themselves instead of the English? Why not own businesses where they could hire other Amish men? Jack also believed that while it was natural that women would take the role of child-rearing, there was no reason why a wife couldn't contribute by working outside the home if the job was in a safe, respectable place. And no reason why a husband couldn't help raising the children God had given him. Unfortunately, the last time Jack had expressed that opinion, his father had gotten so red-faced and angry that Jack had worried he might give himself a heart attack.

Jack shifted his gaze to meet his father's. He was shorter and broader than Jack and wore his graying beard long and untended the way many of the older Amish men did. When Jack married, he decided there and then, that he would wear the beard expected of him, but it would always be neatly trimmed and not so long as to fall into his soup.

His *dat* waited for a response and when Jack didn't say anything, he demanded, "Are you going to come to your senses before you lose every cent of the money your grandfather foolishly loaned you? Money he didn't have to lose?"

Jack was usually quick to lash back at his father when he made comments like that, but for once, he took a breath and thought for a moment. He wouldn't engage with his *dat*. It was too late and Jack was tired. Besides, what would be the point? He went against his father's wishes to start his own business, and nothing he could say or do would gain the older man's approval.

"It was just one bad day, *Dat*," Jack said slowly. "The store will be ready before the deadline. You'll see."

His father grunted and headed for the hall. Halfway there, he stopped. "Talk to Felty again about buying that land of his? He said he'd sell it to you, and then you didn't follow through." His tone was sharp. Judgmental.

"Like I told you, *Dat*—"

"Not that it will matter," his father said, talking over him. "Building houses to sell was a fool's errand to start." He walked out of the room. "Maree!" he snapped, calling Jack's mother's name as he was swallowed into the hallway's darkness. "Time to be abed!"

"*Ya*, coming," she answered obediently as she tucked her darning into its basket. But then she met Jack's gaze as she rose from her chair. "I kept your supper warm. Chicken potpie and buttermilk biscuits. Sit, *sohn,* and I'll bring it to you."

Jack rested his hands on the back of a chair at the table. "*Danki, Mam.* I can get it. You should go before he gets cross with you, too."

Her round face softened, her dark eyes twinkling behind her wireframe eyeglasses. "He means well," she said quietly. "His heart is in the right place. It's only that he worries about you. About your future."

Jack wanted to believe that his father's criticisms were based on concern for his welfare, but when his *dat* said things like what he'd just said, it was hard. He watched his mother pull a plate from the warming drawer beneath her cookstove. "I can do this, *Mam*." He pulled the chair and sat down. "I'm going to build this store. I'll be the most sought-after contractor in Kent County someday," he told her passionately. Because he was passionate about his dream.

"*Ach*, I know you will, *sohn*." She squeezed his shoulder with her hand and slid the plate in front of him. "Do you want to tell me what happened today? Why it didn't go so well?" She retrieved a fork and knife and set them down in front of him.

"*Nay*. I just want to eat and go to bed." He closed his eyes for a moment, gave a silent prayer of thanks and dug into the plate's generous portions of chicken potpie. "Tell me about your day instead. What did you do?"

She returned to the table with the butter dish and a jar of her homemade raspberry jam. His favorite. "The same as every day, *sohn*," she answered cheerfully. "I cooked and cleaned. Ah, but I had visitors today."

Jack tried not to shovel his food into his mouth, but he was so hungry and the potpie was creamy and delicious. And the crust was as flaky and buttery as any he had ever had. "Did you?" He reached for the jar of jam, forgoing the butter and slathered one of the biscuits with jam. "Who was that?"

"Emma and Barbara Troyer. They brought a cinnamon coffee cake."

"Did they?" he asked, keeping his tone in check. A pretty brunette two years younger than him, Barbara Troyer was determined to walk out with him. She was why he'd gotten into such hot water with Willa. He'd been innocent, but Willa hadn't seen it that way, and Barbara had made matters worse by prattling on about dating him to anyone who would listen.

"She asked about you." His mother smiled slyly. "I think she was hoping you'd be home. I saved a piece of her coffee cake for you to have after your supper and another piece to pack for your lunch tomorrow. But tomorrow is Saturday," she said. "Silly me. You don't work on Saturdays. You'll be here helping your *vadder*."

"I'm thinking about working over at the Koffmans' tomorrow. Try to make up for lost time." He took a big bite of the jam-covered biscuit, then another. His mouth was so full that he had to chew and swallow before he added, "I'm hoping *Dat* will let Lemuel come with me. I could use his help."

She nodded and then returned the conversation to her visitors, likely so she wouldn't have to address the fact that it was unlikely his father would give Lem permission to work with Jack. His brother would have to be at his father's bidding as usual on Saturdays. Because Jack had been working in construction for several years for various contractors, his father had gotten used to the idea that his second-born son often had to work six days a week. But Lem wasn't so blessed.

"Barbara asked if we were going to Matt Beachy's house for his mother's birthday supper," his mother said. "Frieda is going to be ninety." She hesitated before going on. "Barbara seemed eager to see you again. Pretty girl. And very attentive to her mother." She rubbed her rough, chapped hands together absently. "I think she's hoping you might ask to take her home some night after a singing or a frolic."

Jack started on the second biscuit. "I won't be taking Barbara Troyer home from the Beachys' or anywhere else."

His mother knitted her thick brows. "Why's that, *sohn*? Her mother said such nice things about you." She hesitated. "Barbara is going to make a fine wife for someone. You'll be twenty-four come fall. It's time you thought about taking a wife and having your own family."

He scraped his plate, not wanting to waste a drop of his mother's chicken gravy. "I'm not marrying Barbara Troyer," he said emphatically.

"Why not?"

Jack hesitated for a moment, not sure how much to say. His mother knew his and Willa's brief relationship hadn't ended well, but she didn't know the details. And she didn't need to know them. "Because that girl is trouble."

And because I've got my eye on another.

Chapter Six

Beth was thankful Saturday morning for the excuse to take an envelope to the mailbox. She needed some fresh air—and to get away from her sisters. All of them.

The day had started well enough, with the sun peeking out from behind clouds and the smell of fresh grass drifting through the windows cracked open an inch in the bedroom she shared with her sisters. Breakfast had been pleasant, with their father content to eat whatever his daughters served. While the kitchen was cleaned up, he'd sat at his chair at the head of the table, slurped his coffee and read aloud tidbits from the latest edition of the *Budget*.

Beth had been getting flour to make noodles to go along with their supper when Cora and Eleanor got into it again about Cora applying for the new teaching position. The other sisters quickly took sides, and before Beth knew it, raised voices echoed in the kitchen.

Beth agreed with Cora that she ought to, at the very least, be allowed to meet with the school board to hear the details of the position. However, she also sympathized with Eleanor. Even though she was a twenty-six-year-old unmarried woman running a household and a farm, she was more traditional than the rest of them. Beth knew it couldn't be easy to make so many decisions in a day, worry about money and their father, whom Eleanor believed she was ultimately responsible for. But then Beth understood Cora's point, as well. Cora wasn't ready to marry and have babies like Millie. Cora had always wanted to teach school and this was her opportunity—before she got married and had too many responsibilities at home. Why wouldn't Eleanor want Cora to have this chance?

"Going to the mailbox!" Beth called above the din of her sisters fussing with each other. No one responded. As she walked past her father, who was still in his chair at the table, she said. "Need anything, *Dat*?"

He squinted as he studied a pile of nails, nuts and screws that Henry had dumped on the newspaper in front of him after he'd finished reading it. He was supposed to sort and place them into baby food jars. He'd only gotten as far as lining the jars up in neat rows and removing their lids. "*Nay.* Not unless you have some cookies on you."

Beth patted her apron pockets. "Sorry. None on me." She leaned down and whispered in his ear. "But maybe when I get back, I can find one for both of us. I might know where Eleanor hid the peanut butter cookies she made yesterday."

Her father grinned and Beth pressed a kiss to his temple before she left the kitchen. Wearing a jacket and headscarf, the envelope in her hand, she took her time walking down the long lane, enjoying the birdsong and the warmth of the May sunshine on her face.

As she passed the line of trees that blocked the view of the store's building site from the house, she was surprised to see a man, his back to her, near one of the framed walls. She could tell he was Amish by his wide-brimmed straw hat, but there was no horse and buggy. *Who would be there on a Saturday?* she wondered. Not Jack or his crew. The agreement had been that they would only work Monday through Friday. Jack had stipulated that in the contract that Beth had carefully gone over. He said he had to be available to work on his family's farm on Saturdays, and then, of course, no Amish worked on the Lord's Day.

Frowning, Beth walked to the road, tucked the envelope into the mailbox and cut across the grass toward the store. She was halfway there when she realized who the man was. Against her will, she felt a flutter of excitement.

Jack.

What was he doing there, though? As she drew closer she thought he'd turn around, but she called out to him when he didn't. *"Guder mariye."*

He turned around and, seeing her, smiled. "'Morning, Beth." He held a pencil in one hand, a small pad of paper in the other. "Look, before you chew me out, let me explain. I know I thought the exterior framing would be done by yesterday, but we had two full days of rain."

"You done talking?" she asked, raising an eyebrow.

He looked confused. *"Ya,"* he said, drawing out the word.

"Goot. Because what I was *going to say* was how great the first floor looks and I can't wait to see the second floor go up. With all four

walls up, I can get a better idea of what it will look like when it's done. I was surprised you were able to work at all yesterday. Thursday afternoon when the rain finally stopped there was so much water around the foundation. I assumed you wouldn't work until Monday."

She couldn't see his eyes because he was wearing sunglasses, but his face suggested he was looking at her suspiciously.

"You're not upset with me?" he asked slowly.

"*Nay.* How could I be upset with you, Jack? A good-looking man like yourself." She had no idea what had possessed her to say such a thing. Maybe just to keep him off-balance? To give him a taste of his own medicine? Or perhaps because she'd never flirted with a boy and Jack seemed like a good candidate.

He stared at her a moment longer, and then a smile crept across his face. "We got a full day in yesterday, even though we had a couple of setbacks." He glanced at the skeletal walls then back at her. "But I'm happy with what's done so far." He lifted his chin, his smile turning mischievous. "Nice dress. I like the green on you. Goes with your red hair."

She couldn't help but smile back, though she felt slightly embarrassed by his compliment. No one had ever said something like that before. And while she reminded herself of how he had treated her sister, his charm was hard to resist. It was as if nothing mattered to him at this moment but her. Being a middle daughter in a large family, nothing was ever solely about her.

"*Danki*," she said, the sound of her voice bold. "But I'm not a redhead."

"*Nay?* Your hair looks red to me. What I can see of it. Redd*ish*." He tilted his head one way and then the other, studying her. "Red blond, I'd say. Blond red, maybe?"

Something about the way he said it made her laugh. This was fun, flirting with him. Suddenly, she understood what Willa and so many other girls in Honeycomb found attractive in Jack. "Our *mam* called it strawberry blond."

"See." He gestured with the pencil he still held in his hand. "She thought it was red. Strawberries are red, *ya*? Strawberry blond makes sense to me."

She cut her eyes at him and then said, "Enough silliness. You want to walk me through what's going to happen next?" She stared at the wall they were standing beside. "I'm guessing you'll have to finish the first floor ceiling before putting up the walls on the second."

He tucked his pencil behind his ear and then slipped the little notepad into his jacket pocket. "Be happy to show you around. I like to talk about my plans out loud. Helps me see things up here." He tapped his temple.

For the next half hour, they walked around the partially constructed building while Jack answered Beth's questions. After they'd walked around twice, they stopped where the front porch would be, and he explained to her the different types of material she could choose for the roof. That conversation led to the energy-efficient windows he wanted to install. Beth was impressed by his knowledge. She didn't understand everything he said, but his clarifications were clear and he was happy to clarify when she didn't understand.

Jack was explaining how he would rough in the staircase to the second floor when Beth heard a horse and wagon flying down the driveway. She and Jack looked up simultaneously and watched Cora pull up at the end of their lane, throwing gravel in every direction, before her sister turned right, then flew down the road.

"Wonder where she's running to in such a hurry," he remarked.

Beth scoffed. "More like who she's running away *from*."

He met her gaze. The sun had gone behind the clouds and he'd removed his dark sunglasses. His eyes were a deep shade of green without so much as a fleck of brown.

Beth hesitated. Eleanor wouldn't like it if she told Jack about her and Cora's argument. Family squabbles were meant to remain within the family, but Jack's older brother had spoken to Cora about the job opening. Maybe Jack would know more about it.

As if sensing her hesitation, he said. "It's *oll recht,* you don't have to tell me. As my mother likes to say, I should mind my own knitting." Again the handsome smile.

Beth laughed at his use of the phrase usually relegated to a woman's world. He had to be a confident man to do so. And then she told him the whole story, including the part his older brother had played in it. Jack listened without interrupting, then asked a couple of questions. He was quiet for a moment before he said, "I understand Eleanor's hesitancy in letting Cora take a job. It's unusual in Honeycomb for a woman to work full-time and have that much responsibility. That's why men usually teach our children."

"But single women work. Liz Yoder works at Fifer's Orchards, and Martha Swartzentruber works at the deli at Spence's Bazaar."

"Hmm." He grimaced. "But neither works full-time. They're still available to work at home with their mothers." He shrugged. "Our bishops are strict. They cling to the old ways."

"Women can teach school," she argued firmly. "Other Amish communities in Kent County have women teachers. Last year Seven Poplars hired Trudy who came from Canada with her family. In some ways, I'd say women are better suited to teaching than men. Women are the ones who take care of the *bopplin* at home. Who knows children better?"

He held up his hands, palms out. "I'm not saying I agree with it, Beth. I understand the quandary our community and many other Old Order communities are finding themselves in. It's all the elders talk about behind closed doors. We walk a fine line as Old Order Amish trying to remain separated from the English world."

He hesitated thoughtfully and then went on. "For a long time, the old ways worked just fine. Women ran the households, cooked and cleaned, worked our gardens, cared for the children and the men ran the farms. My *dat* grew up as his *vadder* had and his *vadder* before him, as we did for generations." He shook his head. "But like it or not, we don't live in that world anymore. Farming doesn't pay enough to support a family. Maybe it does in places where there's more land to be had, but not in Delaware. That's why I wanted to start this contracting business. So I can support a family someday, because farming isn't going to do it. I can't afford to buy the amount of land I'd need and even if I could, Delaware doesn't have that kind of farmland to develop."

His response wasn't what she had anticipated. She had expected him to say that women were meant to be married by Cora's age. That they were meant to be in the kitchen, barefoot with a *boppli* on their hip and another on the way. "So you think it's *oll recht* for women to work outside the home?" she challenged.

He drew his thumb and forefinger down his cleanly shaved chin. "I think it depends on the woman and her situation. I see nothing wrong with Cora, as a single woman, teaching school and contributing to the family household." He shrugged. "If she were married, then she and her husband would be the ones to decide if it was the right thing for their family."

She narrowed her gaze. "You mean it should be her husband's decision."

He frowned. "I didn't say that. I guess it would depend on the marriage. In my parents' house, my *dat* makes the decisions without asking my *mam* anything. But like I said, men and women our age will have to do things differently than our folks did." He met her gaze. "I wouldn't have a problem with my wife working if she wanted to and we could figure out how to make it work."

Jack's modern beliefs shocked Beth into silence. Could this man be the *dummkopf* Willa had dated? He had Beth perplexed but also intrigued. She hadn't known there was a man her age in Honeycomb who believed the same things she did. And if she had known, he would have been the last person she would have guessed would think this way.

Jack glanced away and then back at Beth. "Is that the end of it? If Eleanor says no, Cora won't apply?"

Beth chewed on her lower lip. "I hope not. The fact that the school board would even consider Cora must mean they think she could do it. If your brother asked her about it, I suspect the board already spoke to some of the bishops. The bishops might not have given their approval to hire a woman, but they couldn't have said no, otherwise the board wouldn't have sent Amos to speak to her."

"You want me to ask Amos about it?"

His offer surprised her. "Would you? Maybe you could get some details about the job. Cora doesn't know which school they'd be hiring for. That's part of Eleanor's worry. If it's far enough from here, Cora would need to take our horse and buggy and that would leave us with only the wagon on weekdays during the school year. Eleanor doesn't want us to be stranded with no way to get anywhere in poor weather."

He hooked his thumbs through his leather suspenders. "I'd be happy to talk to Amos. I'll let you know what he says."

"*Danki,*" she said. They were both quiet for a moment.

Beth knew she should go. She'd already taken enough of his time and he said he had more calculations to make before he headed home on his push scooter. "Guess I best get to my chores." She smiled at him. "Thanks for showing me around and answering my foolish questions."

"Not foolish all. They were *gut* ones," he answered. "And like I said, having someone to explain things to makes it all clearer in my mind."

They were smiling at each other again.

"See you next week. I'll be by to see how things are going." She waggled her finger at him. "And make sure you're earning your pay."

He laughed and gave a wave as she walked away. "Come by anytime."

She had taken two steps when he called out to her. "Hey, Beth?"

"*Ya?*" She stopped to look back.

"Your family going to the Beachys' next Saturday? The birthday party for Frieda?"

"I think so."

"What would you say if I asked to take you home after?" He flashed that handsome grin. "Maybe we could ride the long way home…"

She was so shocked that he would ask her to ride home with him that she was tongue-tied, but then she found her voice. "I'd say you were *narrish.*" She tapped her head. "Crazier even than you seem."

Then she walked away, smiling all the way home.

That night, Beth lay in bed staring at the dark ceiling and the beams of moonlight that slipped through the gaps in the curtains, illuminating slivers of the room. Even though she was tired from a long day of spring-cleaning, she couldn't sleep. She kept going over every word she and Jack had shared that morning, every nuance of their conversation. She'd had such a good time with him and felt immensely guilty about that. What kind of person was she to flirt with the man who had broken her sister's heart? Knowing his reputation, she didn't understand how she could feel this way about Jack. Like she could have spent hours with him. Days.

She groaned and pulled a green and white patchwork quilt her mother had made for her up to her chin. She missed her *mam*. She missed her smile and laughter, but what she missed most was her advice right now. Her mother had always had a patient ear for each of her daughters, and no matter how frivolous the concern, she'd always had time to set aside whatever she was doing to listen and offer guidance.

"Can't sleep either?" Jane whispered.

Beth rolled onto her side and propped her head up with her elbow. The bed between her and her little sister was empty. Willa had gone to stay the night with her friend Liz, who was busy making wedding preparations.

"*Nay*," Beth sighed.

"Me either."

Beth watched Jane roll onto her side so they could see each other in the semidarkness. "What's keeping you awake, *schweschter*?"

"*Ach*, I think that second piece of chocolate cream pie I had."

Beth smiled to herself. She wasn't glad her sister had a tummy ache, but it did her heart good to know that Jane, though sixteen going on seventeen and nearly an adult, could still enjoy childish behaviors like eating too much pie. "Want me to get you some bicarbonate?" she asked.

"*Nay*, it's getting better." Jane flipped on the flashlight she kept under her pillow to read at night. She pointed it in Beth's direction. "I saw you with Jack Lehman this morning when I walked to Elden's."

Beth held up her hand to block the beam of light. "Not in my eyes, silly."

Jane lowered the beam to create a puddle of light on Beth's bed. "He seems smitten with you. Jack."

Beth was quick to defend herself. "Why would you say such a thing? We were discussing the construction. He works for me. Us," she added, flustered. What had her sister thought she had seen? Was it that obvious that Beth was attracted to Jack?

But that wasn't what her little sister had said. What she had said was that Jack was smitten *with her*.

"I don't know. The way he looked at you. The way he smiled."

Beth felt a warmth spread through her. *Jack had looked at her as if he liked her*? But the idea of it also made her uncomfortable. "Why were you spying on me?" she asked.

Taking no offense, Jane laughed girlishly. "I wasn't *spying* on you. I walked over to Elden's with Millie. We saw you from the driveway. We waved at you, but neither of you saw us." Again, she giggled. "Maybe because you were too busy gazing into each other's eyes."

Beth didn't know how to respond. Thankfully, Jane kept talking.

"He's very handsome. And he has good job, *ya*? A man like Jack would build his wife a new house, wouldn't he? I can't imagine living in a new house. No leaking roof, no creaky doors. Are you going to walk out with him?"

"*Nay*, I'm not going to walk out with him," Beth said, trying to sound indignant. "Not after what he did to Willa."

"But how do you know what he did to Willa?" her little sister asked, sounding naive.

Beth exhaled impatiently, though her impatience was more with herself and the thoughts of Jack that ran around in her head, keeping her awake than with Jane. "Willa told us what happened."

"Willa told us *her* version of what happened," Jane corrected.

"What are you talking about?"

"Shh," Jane hushed. "If Eleanor hears us, she'll be in here giving us what for. It took her too long to get *Dat* to bed to have us wake him." She flipped off the flashlight and the room grew darker again. "You know *Mam* always told us that each of us sees things differently. You and I could see or hear the same thing but tell the story differently because it's from our eyes."

Beth rolled onto her back. "I have no idea what you mean."

"What I mean is that we don't all see situations the same." She hesitated. "Especially Willa. Remember that time I was carrying all those canning jars up from the cellar and she didn't hold the door open for me and it closed on me and I dropped all the jars and they broke? She told *Mam* that I had dropped the jars, which I did. But she didn't mention that I dropped them because of what she did.

She didn't say it to get me in trouble. It was just her...her reality."

Beth laughed. "Her reality? Where do you get these ideas? What kind of books are you reading under the covers at night? I sure hope it's something our uncle would approve of."

Jane turned the flashlight on again, directing it at Beth. "You're not listening to what I'm saying, Beth. I'm telling you that you heard what Willa thinks happened, but do you know how Jack sees it? Their views might not match up."

As the words came out of Jane's mouth, Beth thought about something Jack had said to her when he'd first started working for them. He'd told her that there were two sides to every story. Was there another side to the story of him and Willa? Had Willa misled her family? Or, as Jane had suggested, had her sister just seen the situation differently? But it was hard to dispute that Jack had been dating Barbara Troyer at the same time he was dating Willa. That had happened. Beth knew Barbara had ridden home not once but at least twice with Jack from events. Everyone in Honeycomb knew she had gone with him.

"You know I love Willa—I adore her," Jane went on. "But she sees things in relationship to herself, not others. She doesn't always see us, Beth." She turned off the flashlight and lay back in her bed. "Just something to think about," she added sleepily.

A short time later, Beth drifted off to sleep wondering, did Jane have a point? What if Willa's reality wasn't Jack's?

Chapter Seven

"I've never seen so many pies," Willa fussed. "I can't believe Ellen thinks we'll eat all of them."

Beth and Willa carried a pie in each hand, moving them from Ellen Beachy's kitchen to the dessert table in the backyard. It was their third trip and they had three more to go. Originally the plan had been to have dessert in the house after the picnic supper, but it was such a warm evening that Ellen decided to continue the celebration outside.

"And whoever heard of pie for a birthday?" Willa continued as she followed Beth. They walked across the back porch and into the backyard where tables had been set up under poplar trees strung with solar café lights. "It's called birthday *cake*, not birthday *pie*. No one wants birthday pie. Not even a ninety-year-old."

Beth smiled to herself. Willa wasn't upset about what Ellen was serving her mother-in-law for her birthday, but that Beth had volunteered her sister's assistance when Ellen had asked Beth to move the pies. As Willa saw it, the more time she spent serving and cleaning up with the women, the less time she had to flirt with the boys.

"Frieda Beachy wanted birthday pie," Beth explained, her gaze lingering on Jack Lehman's broad shoulders as she set down two shoo-fly pies. He stood on the far side of the picnic tables, talking with the Beachy brothers, Matt and Fred, who had thrown the birthday party for their mother. Since Beth's arrival, Jack had tried to get her attention, but she'd ignored him.

A part of Beth wanted badly to talk with Jack. She wanted to be with him. But she also worried it would be wrong to respond to her attraction to him, even though it seemed to be mutual. Why else would Jack have asked her to ride home with him after Frieda's party? Even though Beth saw nothing of the man Willa had painted Jack to be, it seemed wrong to consider riding home with him. Yet she wanted to. Did that make her a bad person?

Beth cut her eyes at her sister as Beth took the two apple crumb pies from her and set them on the table covered in a pink plastic tablecloth. Frieda's favorite color was pink, and Ellen and her sister-in-law Alma had covered all the tables for their fifty guests in pink and used pink paper napkins. Some folks had even worn pink, though Beth hadn't because she didn't own a pink dress.

"What do you care what Frieda has for her birthday?" Beth asked.

"I don't." Willa crossed her arms impatiently. "Can you carry the last couple of pies? Please?" she begged as her gaze flitted to a group of young, single men standing near the milk house trying to pretend they weren't checking out all the single women.

Beth noted that whomever her sister was interested in, thankfully, it wasn't Jack. As terribly as Willa had talked about him, that didn't mean she hadn't changed her mind about him. Willa was fickle that way. One minute she couldn't stand a boy and then the next thing, she was flirting with him. "Have something better to do?" Beth asked, her tone teasing.

Willa smiled mischievously and whispered, "See the tall one in the pink shirt?"

Beth didn't know him, but she guessed, by

the looks of him, that he was a Beachy relative. Fred and Matt had six brothers and five sisters in Ohio and one family or the other was always sending a son or a daughter to visit Honeycomb with the hopes of them meeting a potential spouse. "Is he the one with the really big nose?" Beth teased, pretending to squint to get a better look.

Willa elbowed her sister. "He does not have a big nose. His nose fits his face." Smiling coyly, she glanced at the young man again. "His name's John Mary."

"Beachy?" Beth asked, arranging the pies on the table and setting serving utensils beside each one. "One of Fred and Matt's nephews?"

"*Ya.* Their brother Eli's son. His oldest. Jane said she heard he was apprenticing as a mason back in Ohio." Willa smiled dreamily. "He has nice hands. I love a man's hands. I can see myself marrying a mason. I imagine he'd build us a big brick house."

Beth glanced at her. "You better not let Eleanor hear you saying you want to marry and move to Ohio. You heard her this morning. She said we should all marry men who live here in Kent County to stay close to *Dat.*"

"So maybe John Mary wants to move to Honeycomb and that's why he's visiting. There's a lot of construction around here. Plenty of work for a mason. Maybe Jack would give him a job."

Beth didn't make eye contact with her sister. "This mean your heart's mended after the breakup with Jack?"

Willa didn't answer. She was too busy waving at John Mary. Which Beth could assume meant Willa *was* over Jack. Did that mean Willa would be okay with it if she rode home with him tonight?

"Look at him," Willa whispered. "Isn't he the cutest? I wonder if he'd be able to borrow a buggy from his uncle to take me home. Or maybe he could walk me home. A walk in the moonlight."

"A walk in the moonlight with a chaperone, maybe. I imagine *Dat* wouldn't mind walking home with you."

Willa stuck her tongue out at Beth, and Beth laughed. It was good to see Willa back to her old self. It didn't seem as if it had been that long since she'd dated Jack, but maybe her heart had been more bruised than broken.

"So are you going to go talk to him, or are you just going to stand there and make goo-goo eyes at him?" Beth asked.

Willa's face lit up as she looked at Beth. "You'll carry the rest of the pies out yourself?"

"*Ya.* Or grab someone else to help." Beth walked away. "Go on."

"*Danki*!" Willa called over her shoulder as she ambled toward the young man.

Beth made three more trips with pies before she crossed paths with Jane, and together they carried the last of them. When the sun set, Fred and Matt gathered their guests around their mother, seated in a lawn chair, and everyone sang happy birthday in English. Frieda grinned toothlessly, clapping her hands, and insisted they sing the song again. Then Ellen offered her mother-in-law the first piece of pie, and when Frieda couldn't choose, she ended up with an entire dinner plate of various slices to sample.

A short time later, Beth was standing outside the circle of light cast by the café lights overhead, finishing a slice of lemon curd pie, when she heard a voice behind her.

"Like to go for a walk?"

Her heart fluttered. She didn't have to turn to see who it was. She knew his voice.

Jack moved to her side, took her paper plate and disposable fork, and dropped them into a trash can.

"Hey," she protested. "What if I wanted another piece of pie?"

He grabbed her hand, and before she could

protest, led her deeper into the darkness. "I know I do. When we get back, we'll have another piece."

She resisted being pulled along, but not in earnest. "What if there isn't any more apple crumb left?"

He stopped to face her, her hand still in his. "Then you'll choose another, Beth."

His touch made her feel off-kilter, as if she'd been spinning in circles, then stood still the way she and her sisters had when they were little girls. It wasn't an unpleasant feeling. It made her face flush and her heart beat a little faster.

But what would Jack think of her if she let him hold her hand? It wasn't as if they were walking out together. And what if someone saw them and told Eleanor? Eleanor was constantly reminding her sisters that as a household of young women without a proper guardian, they must behave in a way that the church elders would never see as improper. The rules on dating in Honeycomb had eased over the last few years, but there were still families that would not allow their daughters to walk out with a boy without a chaperone.

Beth slipped her hand out of Jack's. "Why are we going for a walk?"

"Because I want to talk to you." He glanced

in the direction of the picnic tables under the lights. Everyone was milling around, eating pie, laughing, talking and offering Frieda well-wishes as she ate heartily from her plate. "Without an audience."

Beth fell into step beside him. "Is it about the store? Is there a problem? I thought you said everything was going well. That you caught up this week and then some and planned to shingle the roof next."

He held up a low-lying branch for her to duck under as they followed a path toward the Beachy family's pond. Though it had grown quite dark, it was easy to find their way because there were tiny solar lights staked in the ground every few feet.

"I thought we could talk about something other than the store for once," Jack said.

"Why?" she asked. Which was a silly thing to say because it was apparent. He wanted to walk with her because he liked her. And she suspected he knew the feeling was mutual. She twisted her hands together nervously and kept walking.

"I already told you. I like you, Beth. And I want to take you home tonight."

She kept walking. "You like me?" she asked, her tone turning terse. "The same way you liked Willa?"

He groaned, sliding his hands into his pockets and lowering his head. "*Nay*, not the same. With you, it feels different…" He hesitated. "I can't stop thinking about you, Beth. I've gone over our conversations, wondering where you are and what you're doing. Worrying you'll walk out with someone else before you give me a chance."

Once again, she found it easier to be quarrelsome with him than deal with her growing feelings for him. "Are you just saying all that so I'll ride home with you?"

"Beth—"

"Maybe you ought to ask Barbara Troyer to ride home with you instead," she interrupted.

He stopped and looked down at his boots. She halted in front of him, immediately regretting what she had said. It was unkind and she wasn't a mean person. It was only that… that she really liked him. And she didn't want to. And maybe if she were mean enough, he'd leave her alone.

But, of course, that wasn't what she wanted. Beth wanted to ride home with him tonight under the stars. She wanted to sit beside him in his wagon and listen to the night sounds of insects and nocturnal animals and talk. She'd never met a boy before whom she could talk to so easily. And not just about the store, but other things, too. The fact that he believed, as she did, that their generation had to adapt to keep their way of life had been eye-opening and exciting. And that he agreed that there was a place in an Amish woman's life for working outside the home had made her like him even more. Maybe too much.

"I'm sorry," she murmured. "That wasn't nice."

He was quiet for a moment and then, his tone mischievous, he said, "It's not like I *could* ask Barbara Troyer. She's not here."

Beth smiled at his joke but refused to be redirected. She knew the technique firsthand—she used it with her father all the time. "I need to ask you something, Jack. Something serious."

"Go ahead."

She took a breath, exhaled and, before she chickened out, she said, "Exactly what happened with you and Willa?"

He grimaced. "I think I'd rather talk about the store."

She went on. "Weeks ago you told me that there were two sides to every story. I want to know your side."

"Shall we walk to the pond?" He pointed. "We're almost there. Matt said he added a bench on the dock. He built it because he and Ellen like to come down after supper and have a few moments to themselves. I like the idea of that. A couple married as long as Ellen and Matt have been and he still likes to take walks with his wife. I want that kind of marriage."

Beth had never heard a young man talk so romantically about marriage. But she couldn't let that distract her from the issue of Willa and the things Willa had accused him of. Or the things her friend Rosie had said about his reputation.

"*Oll recht,* I'll walk down to the pond with you. But I'm serious. I need to know what happened between you and my sister."

He slid his hands into his pockets and they walked again. Someone had mowed the path but the grass and weeds were a foot tall on either side and were fragrant and thick. She heard chirping crickets and croaking frogs all around them.

"I'm not sure I feel right talking to you about Willa," Jack said slowly. "You should ask her what happened."

"I've already heard her version. I want to know what you think happened."

He frowned and glanced at her as they walked side by side. "What happened is what happened. Is there a version?"

"You were the one who said there were two

sides of the story," she pressed. "I know what Willa and other people are saying. If you want me to ride home with you tonight, you have to tell me *your* side of the story."

"And if I do, you'll ride home with me?"

"I haven't decided yet," she said, imitating the coy tone she'd heard in Willa's voice when she talked to boys.

They reached the edge of the dock and went to the bench, their footsteps sounding on the wooden boards and echoing over the water. Solar lamps attached to the dock cast circles of light onto the rippling pond and it was easy for Beth to see her way and take a seat.

Jack eased down beside her and stretched out his long legs. When he spoke, his tone was solemn. "I don't know exactly what Willa told you, but I've heard what other people are saying. Gossip has a way of making stories a lot more...*interesting* than they often are." He took a deep breath. "You really want to hear this?"

"*Ya*, I do." Beth folded her hands in her lap. They were sitting so close that she could smell his shaving soap, yet not so close that they were touching.

"Willa and I had a big argument one night when we went to a singing in the matchmaker's barn in Seven Poplars."

"About what?" Beth asked.

He shrugged. "You know, honestly, I'm not even sure now. I imagine she thought I was flirting with someone. She was always accusing me of flirting with other girls."

"And were you?" Beth pressed.

"Maybe sometimes. Before we were dating, but not during. I wouldn't do that. But I can't help it if a girl flirts with me." He scratched at a spot on his pants. "Anyway, Willa was furious with me. So furious that she broke up with me and rode home with Silas Yost, who she had been flirting with earlier in the evening with me standing right beside her."

Beth eyed him. She remembered the night Willa and Jack had gone to matchmaker's singing. She had no idea her sister had broken up with Jack that night or ridden home with Silas. Beth had assumed Jack had brought her home. "Willa broke up with you at the matchmaker's?"

"She did. She said she never wanted to see me again. So I drove home from Seven Poplars alone. The next day after church I tried to talk to her but she refused. She said she wasn't speaking to me ever again." He exhaled loudly. "So I assumed we were broken up and... and a week or so later I ran into Barbara Troyer at

Spence's Bazaar and we talked. She was nice enough, and—" he shrugged "—and so I drove her home from one event or another. But only three times and we never went out on a date."

"*Oll recht.*" Beth drew out the last word.

"Then Willa comes up to me at a singing, crying, and she says I cheated on her with Barbara."

Beth tried to process what he was saying. "So Willa said you had cheated on her, but that doesn't make sense if she broke up with you."

"That's what *I* said," Jack exclaimed, coming to his feet, his arms open wide. "But Willa said she hadn't really broken up with me when she said it and I knew it." He stood in front of her, pushing his straw hat farther back on his head. "Except that I didn't know that, because I thought when a girl tells you she's never going to speak to you again, that's the end of the matter. So that night she broke up with me a second time. For real, I guess."

Beth sat back on the bench, her thoughts flying in a hundred directions. Everything Jack said was utterly plausible, and as much as she hated to think it, it sounded like something Willa might do. Yet Willa had seemed upset. Would she have been that upset if things had happened the way Jack said they had?

Beth met his gaze. "Are you dating Barbara Troyer now?"

He made a face. "Barbara? *Nay.* If I were dating Barbara, I wouldn't be asking to take you home. Why would you say such a thing? I just told you, I like you, Beth." He motioned with his chin. "You're the one I want to walk out with."

She shrugged. "I'm just checking. Barbara's a pretty girl and the only daughter. She might have a dowry of some sort."

"I'm not dating Barbara and I told you what happened between your sister and me," Jack said. "So… will you let me drive you home tonight?"

Beth stood, unsure how she would respond until the words came out of her mouth. "Not tonight." Because she needed to think this through. She walked off the dock and onto the path that led back to the Beachys' yard.

"Not tonight?" he called after her. "Does that mean you might say yes next time I ask you?"

When she didn't answer he called into the dark. "Can you give a man hope?"

"There's always hope," Beth called back. And then she walked back to the party, smiling.

Chapter Eight

Beth stood on the porch, her back pressed against the house's exterior wall so she couldn't be seen from the kitchen windows. When the back door opened, she held her breath, afraid her father had seen her slip out. Thankfully, it was only Willa.

"Did he see me leave?" Beth whispered, grabbing her sister's hand.

Willa shook her head. "*Nay.* I didn't even have to distract him. He was playing with the cat. Trying to teach her to sit when he tells her."

Beth covered her mouth and giggled. "How was it going?"

"About how you'd think."

They both laughed. Beth slipped her arm through Willa's and they went down the porch steps together.

"He's so determined," Beth said, "that I won't be surprised if he has that cat sitting when she's told by suppertime."

Willa wiped at her eyes as her merriment subsided. "Sometimes I feel bad laughing at *Dat* like this."

"Don't be," Beth advised. "Were not laughing *at* him. We're laughing at the situation we've all found ourselves in since *Dat*'s diagnosis. "You remember that day right before *Mam* died when *Dat* picked flowers for her and put them in a vase of milk? *Mam* laughed until she cried, and he laughed with her when he realized what he'd done. Later, *Mam* told us girls to never lose our sense of humor with him. She said it was always better to laugh than to cry. And she didn't want us crying about *Dat*'s dementia because she was sure *Gott* wasn't done with him yet and that there was a reason he was the way he was."

Willa smiled nostalgically. "*Mam* was always wise. I wish I were more like her."

"But you're wise, too," Beth said.

Willa smirked. "*Ya, recht.* I'm a lot of things, but wise isn't one of them." She glanced around as they walked down their lane toward the road. "It's nice to get out of the house. It's a beautiful day."

And it was. The sun shone and the sky was blue and cloudless. It was a perfect day for construction work, which was why Beth had sneaked out of the house. She felt guilty about going to the store without their *dat*, but there was a lightheartedness to her step. It was as if she and Willa were girls again and slipping out to play when they were supposed to be doing chores. Only now Beth was going to see a man. To see Jack. No, she wasn't going to see him, she told herself. She was going to check how the building was progressing. If Jack happened to be there and they spent some time talking, so be it.

Not wanting to think about Jack and the confusing feelings bubbling up inside her, Beth turned the subject back to their father."I still can't believe Ellie gave in and let *Dat* bring that cat in the house."

"I think she didn't so much agree to it as she gave up trying to keep it out," Willa explained. "Last night when she went into *Dat*'s bedroom to check on him, she found it on his bed. She couldn't figure out how he got it past her after watching him carry it outside after supper. Turns out he *did* take the cat out, but then he walked around the house, opened his bedroom window and dropped her inside so Ellie was none the wiser."

The sisters laughed again.

"He does love that cat," Willa went on. "I asked him this morning if he wanted to go to Elden's with me. You know how much he likes Elden's bulldog, Winston. But *Dat* wanted to take the cat. He refused to go when I told him we couldn't take it because Lavinia dislikes cats."

Willa was headed across the street to join Millie to help her put up new curtains in the *dawdi h*ouse Elden had built for his mother in their backyard. When he and Millie married, Lavinia would move into the small, single-story home to allow Elden and Millie to have the farmhouse to themselves.

Beth was going down to the store to see what Jack and his crew had done over the last couple of days. She had avoided Jack since they had talked at the Beachys', giving herself some time to think about him and what to do. She thought she'd already known what she wanted, but she had to be sure. She was sure now, which was why she'd suggested that she and Willa walk to the end of the lane together.

Realizing they had nearly reached the road, Beth took a deep breath. If she was going to talk to Willa about Jack today, she had to do it now. "I have a question for you," she said before she lost her nerve. "And please promise me you'll be honest, Willa. I would never hurt your feeling on purpose."

Willa cut her eyes at her sister suspiciously. *"Oll recht."*

"I was wondering if…if—" Beth stopped and started again. This was harder than she'd thought it would be. Not just because of the question she needed to pose but because it would be a declaration of her interest in Jack. "I was wondering…" She couldn't get the words out.

"What is wrong with you?" Willa stared at her.

Beth felt her face growing flushed. "Would you care if I walked out with Jack Lehman?" she blurted.

Willa halted. "Jack?" she asked in disbelief.

Beth couldn't make eye contact with her sister.

"Wait a minute. Is that why you two left the party the other night?" Willa asked. "Because you two are secretly dating?"

"*Nay*, absolutely not. We're not dating. And we didn't leave the party," Beth explained. "We…we went for a walk." She pressed her hand to her mouth. "*Ach*, I didn't realize anyone saw us go."

"Oh, people saw you, *oll recht*. You know Honeycomb. No one misses anything in this town. Though mostly it was the girls who took notice, wishing Jack would ask *them* to take a walk."

Beth was quiet as she waited for Willa to answer her question, hoping she wouldn't be forced to repeat it.

Thankfully, as Willa started walking again, she said, "I don't care if you walk out with him. He's not my beau anymore. You can have him." Her frown turned into a smile of delight. "Did you hear that John Mary Beachy asked me to meet him at the singing at Aunt Judy and Uncle Cyrus's on Friday night? John Mary is so handsome and sweet. I think he could be the one," she murmured, as much to herself as to her sister.

Beth hadn't realized she'd been holding her breath until she released it. She had known she had to ask Willa about Jack, but she didn't know what she would have done if Willa had said she *didn't* want her to walk out with him. She'd like to think she could have ended whatever was simmering between her and Jack, but she was glad she wouldn't have to find out.

Beth had considered asking Willa to explain again what had happened with Jack but decided against it. What good would it do if Willa's recollection was the same as before? Beth wasn't going to accuse Jack or her sister of telling lies. As Jane had pointed out, maybe what they had said was the truth from their respective points of view. Instead she repeated the question so she was certain of the answer. And to be sure that Willa remembered her answer later. "Are you sure it's okay?"

"You know me better than that, *schweschter*. I wouldn't say it's okay if it's not." They reached the paved blacktop where they would part, with Willa crossing to Elden's property and Beth veering off to cross the grass to the store. "But I'm warning you," Willa continued. "No matter how charming and good-looking Jack is, he's not worth having. All he'll do is break your heart like he broke mine." She waved as she crossed the road. "See you at home later."

"See you later, *schweschter*."

Beth made her way to the store, where she found Rosie's brother Mark and Jack's brother Lem nailing sheets of plywood onto the exterior walls to close in the structure. Jack was cutting the boards for them. When he saw her walking toward them, he turned off the battery-operated saw and strode toward her, greeting her with a big grin.

"There you are. I was beginning to wonder what happened to you," he said. "We were here all day Monday and again yesterday, but you never showed up."

She crossed her arms. Her first impulse was to be contrite with him, though she didn't know why. "Are you saying you need me to *supervise* you?"

He chuckled, pushing back the brim of his straw hat to reveal more of his handsome, suntanned face. "I'm saying I missed you, Beth."

She couldn't see his eyes because he wore wrap sunglasses, but he sounded sincere. She felt herself blush. "I've been busy is all."

"And not avoiding me?" He tilted his head questioningly.

She looked down at her bare feet. "Of course not. Why would I avoid you?"

"Good point. I'm too adorable to be ignored, *ya*?" he teased.

She smiled, unable to meet his gaze. She could feel her cheeks growing even warmer with embarrassment. She wasn't good at this flirting thing, but it *was* fun. She dared a peek at him. "I don't know that I'd go that far," she returned.

He laughed. "Well, I'm glad you're here. I want to show you a couple of things. Just let me cut one more sheet of plywood." They walked side by side. "Where's Felty? I'm surprised you got away from the house without him."

"I didn't exactly get away without him," she admitted sheepishly. "I sneaked out of the house so he wouldn't know I'd left again."

Jack slid a pair of protective goggles over his sunglasses and reached for his saw. "Well, I'm afraid to tell you it didn't work."

"What?" she asked.

He lifted his chin in the direction of the house. "Here he comes. Ready for work." Then he flipped on the saw and the sound prevented any further conversation.

Beth turned around to see her father cutting across the grassy field. He was dressed for work in his steel-toe boots from his days as a mason and a battered straw hat. He carried an old toolbox. "Oh, *Dat*," she sighed.

By the time Jack had cut the board and switched off the saw, her father had reached them.

"Sorry I'm late. Had a cat to attend to," he told Jack. "What do you want me to do? Cut?" He pointed at the saw Jack had just set down.

Jack removed his safety goggles. "Don't need any more plywood cut right now. I could use some help organizing the lumber that was delivered this morning, though." He pointed at a pile. "I need some help to take inventory. I'm afraid they delivered an order meant for someone else."

Her father studied the pile of lumber for a moment, set down his toolbox and walked away.

Jack stood beside Beth as they watched the older man pick up at two-by-four and set it aside in the grass. "I know you're not one to give up easily, Beth, but I think you're fighting a losing battle here," he said without looking at her.

She chuckled.

"So why not try it?" Jack suggested. "Let your *dat* stay a few hours. It's going to get up to eighty degrees today. Maybe he'll decide coming out of retirement wasn't such a good idea after all."

Jack was right and Beth knew it, but she hated to admit it because that would mean he knew what her father needed better than she did. It was a hard thing to concede when she and Jack had started at such odds. "I have work to do at the house," she argued half-heartedly.

"I don't have time to watch him move wood from one pile to another."

"I'll keep an eye on him," Jack assured. "You know I will."

Her resolve crumbled as she watched her father cheerfully carry another length of lumber. "You won't let him do anything dangerous? Him getting near any power equipment isn't a good idea. Too dangerous. He never used them much, and now…" She let her sentence go unfinished.

"Beth, I'll take good care of him." Jack turned to her. "Leave him here a couple of hours and come back for him at lunchtime. I imagine he'll be tired and have had his fill by then." He shrugged. "One day here and he'll likely never ask to work for me again."

She exhaled and threw up her hands. "Fine."

He took off his sunglasses to meet her gaze. "Fine as in *ya*, you'll let him stay?"

"He can stay until lunch." She waggled her finger at him. "But he better be right here when I get back. You know he wanders."

"I'll take care of him as if he was my own *dat*. Better," Jack promised, his tone sincere. "I'll keep him so busy that he won't have time to think about making a run for it."

"*Oll recht*, but you have to keep an eye on

him. He seems good today, but sometimes he does foolish things." She hesitated. "Thank you, Jack, for doing this for my *dat*. It will mean a lot to him." She paused and added, "It means a lot to me."

"Enough to let me take you on a date?" he asked, his green eyes sparkling with mischief.

"Don't push it." She tried not to smile back at him but failed.

Jack lowered his head as if greatly disappointed. "Can't blame a man for trying. Now come see the walls around the back. And then you need to leave us men to our work."

When he smiled at her again, Beth felt her heart flutter. She was touched by his kindness to her father and his willingness to take on the heavy responsibility of keeping an eye on him.

She thought to herself, a man like this is the kind I always dreamed of marrying.

Jack helped his crew get the last piece of plywood up on the first story and then asked Mark and Lem to set up the lift he'd borrowed to start on the second story after lunch. While they took care of that, he checked on Felty, who was walking the house's perimeter with a large magnet roller to pick up stray nails on a construction site.

Not yet sixty, the older man had good stamina. Since his arrival, he'd been working and only taking a water break when Jack insisted. After Beth had left, Felty had sorted all the lumber, stacking like boards together. He'd then helped Jack count the wood and discovered that they had, indeed, received the wrong order. Jack got the matter straightened out after twenty minutes on his cell phone, mostly on Hold. He was promised a new delivery in the morning and was told to use any lumber he needed from what was delivered and they'd figure out the cost later.

"You want to take a break?" Jack asked Felty.

"Don't need a break." Felty continued to roll the powerful magnet through the grass. "A lot of work to get done here."

"But it's almost lunch. Your daughter will be back for you soon. One of your daughters," Jack corrected, hoping it would be Beth.

She sure had him confused. One minute she spoke to him sternly, the next she graced him with the most beautiful smile he'd ever seen. He thought she liked him, but he couldn't be absolutely sure. Usually, he could tell—girls smiled a lot at him and giggled and hung on every word he spoke. But not Beth.

And maybe that was what intrigued him

about her. She seemed different than the other girls he'd been taking home from singings or dating. Beth was more mature, but in a good way. She had a good head on her shoulders. She listened to him and was interested in what he had to say. Their conversations were never one-sided like they were with other women. Beth had questions and opinions, and she didn't hesitate to share them with him.

The woman was trouble. Jack could see that. After the disaster with Willa, he knew the smart thing to do was to stay away from the Koffman girls. He needed to attend county events for single Amish men and women and meet a nice girl that way. The problem was that he couldn't stop thinking about Beth. He didn't *want* to meet anyone else. He wanted to get to know her better to a level he'd never reached with any other woman he'd known in his past.

Though Jack had always accepted he would marry someday, he hadn't been in any hurry. He liked playing the field. He liked the flirting and the fun that came with being single. But these days, the idea of driving one more girl he didn't know home from a frolic was almost more than he could stomach. Because he'd found himself daydreaming of marriage. He thought about building a little house that he could add to as his family grew. He thought about building a house for the one girl he ought to stay clear of. Beth.

Jack heard her call out as if his thoughts had conjured her up.

"*Dat*. What are you doing?"

Jack looked up to see her walking toward him. On one arm she carried a basket, in the other a glass jug. When she saw him, she lit up with a smile, making him grin. He hurried to take the jug, which was lemonade. The glass was wet with condensation and there were slices of lemons floating in the cold liquid.

"Picking up nails these boys dropped. Mostly good ones," Felty told his daughter as he disappeared around the corner of the building.

"Back so soon?" Jack quipped to Beth.

She sighed with feigned exasperation. "*Someone* has to keep an eye on you. Otherwise, you'll waste away the day napping under one of our trees and not a thing will get done on our store." She held up the basket. "I brought you cookies."

"You made me cookies?" He leaned down and practically stuck his nose in the basket.

She pulled it back from him. "I didn't say I made them, did I? What makes you think I have time to bake cookies for you?" She arranged the cloth napkin over them. "Jane made them. Apparently, she thinks you're handsome."

"And you don't?" he teased. It was a game he often played with single women. He said outrageous things and they were usually entertained by them. At first, Beth had seemed immune to his charm, but he felt she was warming up to him.

"You want the cookies or not?" she asked, resting a hand on her hip. "They're like chocolate chip cookies, only Jane put M&M's in them instead.

"Of course I want them." He held out his hand for the basket. "Let me take that, too. You want one? We could sit under a tree and eat the whole basket."

"I told Eleanor I'd be right back with *Dat*." She walked with him toward Mark's truck. "His lunch is ready and then she wants him to rest. She was none-too-happy I left him here with you."

Jack set the lemonade and the basket on the tailgate. "He's been great, Beth. He really has. He seems to like tidying up, and he hasn't gotten near a single power tool." He poked around in the basket and plucked out a cookie that was nearly as big as his hand. "Wow, these look delicious."

"They're not all for you, mind you. Some are for Mark and Lem. There are jelly jars in the basket, too, for the lemonade." She spotted her father again. "Time to go home, *Dat*!" she called.

"Almost done!"

Beth returned her attention to Jack. "Leave the basket and jug inside the store. One of us will grab it later."

Jack couldn't stop looking at her. She was barefoot and wore a grass-green dress with a white apron. The scarf on her head was tied at the nape of her neck, allowing wisps of her reddish-blond hair to fall forward to frame her pretty face.

"You going to let him come back tomorrow?" He took a bite of the cookie and, of course, it was delicious. Everything the Koffman girls made was delicious, although Jane sometimes used odd ingredients. "I think he'd like it and, honestly, I could use the help. I've been trying to hire another guy to work for me, but I haven't found anyone close enough to get here on his own so far. I don't have time to run my wagon all over town to pick up my crew every day."

She crossed her arms. "I'll have to see what *Dat* has to say about that. And my sister. Sometimes I think she's overprotective of him, but her heart is in the right place."

"*Ya*, I understand. I think I told you that my grandpa had dementia and, at first, my *mam* was afraid to let him out of her sight. She didn't want him in the barns or out in the fields for fear of getting hurt, but she relaxed once she saw that we'd never let anything happen to *Grossdaddi*."

Beth stood there for a moment, looking as if she was going to say something else before she turned away. "I best fetch *Dat* before we're in trouble for letting our lunch sit out." She started to walk away, then called over her shoulder, "Ask me again."

He'd just taken a big bite of cookie and his mouth was full. "What's that?" he choked.

Her smile was saucy. "You heard me. Ask me again. To ride home with you. My aunt and uncle are hosting a singing Friday night. I promised Jane we would go. I'm not much for singings, but Eleanor finally said Jane's old enough to go." Again the smile. "I'll have to get home some way."

He swallowed hard. Her boldness had taken him by surprise. He was used to being the one who asked. But he liked it. "Will you ride home with me from the singing Friday night?"

She turned her head slightly as if thinking hard on the proposition. It took her so long to reply that he began to wonder if this was a setup for her to tell him no, she wouldn't ride home with him. Not if he was the last single man in the county.

Instead, she smiled and said, "I think I will, Jack."

He was still grinning when she and her father had reached the lane and turned for home.

Chapter Nine

Two weeks later, Beth glanced around to search for Jack. He was supposed to have met her at the singing two hours ago. She had agreed to attend the frolic at Mast's Orchards to chaperone Jane, but Jack had offered to join Beth there and then take her home so they could spend time together. The Friday-afternoon picnic meant for singles had started with a game of softball, boys against the girls, then there had been singing after the meal of fried chicken with an assortment of cold salads.

While Beth enjoyed the fast hymns they sang at such gatherings, she'd barely been able to keep up with the songs while watching for Jack. He had promised to meet her there after getting cleaned up after work, but she'd expected him nearly two hours ago. It was getting late enough now that it was time to think about getting Jane home. As a young woman who wasn't dating yet, she wasn't supposed to stay as late as those actively looking for a spouse.

Where was Jack?

Since they'd begun seeing each other two weeks ago, he'd always been where he said he would be. Each time they agreed to see each other. However, Beth still feared that he wouldn't show up. Why would he when he could have his pick of the single women in Honeycomb? There were so many available pretty girls who were far less independent and more agreeable than she was. Even after two weeks of seeing him nearly every day, Beth couldn't figure out why he would choose her.

Returning her attention to the group of girls she was standing with, Beth listened to Esther Krupp talk about her recent betrothal to a man from Kentucky. Before the engagement, Esther and her intended had met only once when she had attended a cousin's wedding the previous fall. Their courting had taken place by mail, but Esther didn't seem to mind that they had not spent any time alone together until he had come to Delaware by train to ask her father for her hand in marriage. Esther beamed with excitement as she talked, then blushed when one of the girls asked for details of the proposal. Esther was obviously head over heels for her fiancé and Beth was happy for her.

Beth was also a bit envious because thoughts of marriage had already crossed her mind after a short time dating Jack. And the more she tried *not* to think about a future with him, the more she daydreamed about it. Courtships were brief in their community, and couples were encouraged to marry quickly without the long engagements the English often had. With the common ground of faith between a man and a woman baptized in the Amish faith, it was believed that love would come with time.

Although marriage was supposed to be the ultimate goal of dating within the Amish community, Beth had told herself the first time she rode home with Jack that she only wanted to have fun. The community of Honeycomb did not allow their young men and women to participate in *rumspringa* as many less restrictive Amish communities did. However, if she *had* been permitted to sow her oats the way her Lancaster County second cousins did, walking out with a man like the flirtatious, fun-loving Jack Lehman was what she would have wanted to do before settling for a more appropriate partner. One who had not dated and broken her sister's heart.

The problem was that the more Beth got to know Jack, the more she saw what a complicated man he was. And the more she liked him. Yes, he was flirtatious and projected a laid back attitude, but he was also intelligent and capable and possessed a deep-thinking side. Since the night Jack had driven her home from her aunt and uncle's, they had seen each other almost every day at the store and had been out together four times. She had never once seen him flirt with another girl in those last two weeks, though many tried to catch his eye. Jack was attentive to Beth whenever they were together without suffocating her, and he seemed to enjoy her company genuinely.

"Beth."

Lost in her thoughts, it wasn't until her sister Millie spoke her name a second time that she realized all the girls in the group were waiting for a response.

Millie touched Beth's arm. "Esther asked you how things were going with you and Jack."

"Um, fine," Beth said, flustered. All eyes were on her and it made her nervous. "It's not anything official, we're just… He's…very nice."

"And so handsome." Millie's friend Annie Lapp giggled behind her hand. "I heard the matchmaker in Seven Poplars has gotten a dozen proposals for him from mothers looking for matches for their daughters. Mothers from as far away as California."

"Who cares about girls in California?" Mary Jane Yoder planted her hands on her hips, obviously put out. "I can't believe you stole him right out from under me, Beth. I was certain he would ask to take me home that night at Bishop Cyrus's and the next thing I know, you're getting into his buggy."

"No need to go on, Maryjane. You weren't going anywhere with Jack Lehman whether he asked you or not," Mary Jane's twin sister Martha Jane chastised. "*Mam* told us we were under no circumstances to accept a ride home from that boy. He's not to be trusted." Her nose upturned, she settled her gaze on Beth. "After what he did to your sister, we're surprised you'd be seeing him."

"That's not a nice thing to say," Millie told the other girl. "You ought to apologize. You're supposed to be Beth's friend."

"It's fine," Beth said quietly, not making eye contact with anyone. She liked Mary Jane and

Martha Jane Yoder, but the girls could be judgmental, and their words weren't always kind.

"I'm sure it's not true, but I heard Jack's still dating Barbara Troyer," Dinah Beachy declared. "Once a two-timer, always a two-timer, that's what my *mam* said."

"You should talk," Annie quipped, eyeing Dinah. "There have been rumors about you going out for late-night walks with someone other than Albert. And here you were telling us you expected to be betrothed soon." She offered a quick smile that didn't seem quite genuine. "Of course, I'm sure it's not true."

Dinah's eyes widened and she glanced over her shoulder as if someone behind her might be listening to the conversation. "Where did you hear that?" she whispered.

The girls' voices faded as Beth scanned the crowd again. Where *was* Jack? she wondered.

Had he changed his mind about wanting to see her?

The talk between the girls had made her nervous. There were so many ways her relationship with Jack could end. If it even was a relationship. He hadn't asked her if he could court her. There had been no talk of being boyfriend and girlfriend. For all she knew, she might only be a diversion for him while he waited for a better choice to come along. No matter how much fun she had with him, a part of her knew it wouldn't last. As her mother used to say, when something looks too good to be true, it probably isn't.

So maybe Jack wasn't coming. Maybe she should stop looking for him and round up her sisters and head home. There was no need to wait around.

Beth was about to tell Millie it was time to find Jane and head home when she saw Jack hurrying across the Masts' backyard toward her. He had changed from his work clothes and wore clean denim pants, a blue shirt with sleeves rolled up to his elbows and good suspenders. When he caught her eye, he grinned and raised his hand in greeting.

Beth's plan of going home with her sisters melted away. She stepped back from the clutch of girls who had spotted him, too. Some of them giggled as if they were still schoolgirls rather than young women ready to marry and raise families.

Seeing Jack striding toward her, his eyes solely on her, made Beth's heart beat faster. It was true what Annie had said; he *was* such a handsome man. But Beth barely noticed his chiseled good looks anymore. When she thought of him, she focused on the person he was, not his striking appearance. She admired his determination to build a business despite his father's doubts that he could do it. She was fascinated by how his brain worked. He wasn't just smart; he could figure things out. And he was kind to her father. For that reason alone, she adored him. Since the first day her *dat* had joined Jack's work crew, Felty had gone every day. And each day, Jack insisted that not only was her *dat* not a problem, but that he was also a great help.

"I'm sorry I'm so late," Jack said as he walked up to her.

The girls grew quiet and Beth could feel them watching her and Jack as they tried to eavesdrop on their conversation.

"My *dat*'s driving horse threw a shoe on my way home from your place and he insisted the gelding be reshod immediately."

"I'm sorry to hear that," Beth said. "Is the horse *oll recht*?

"He's fine. Does anyone in your family have a cell phone? I felt bad leaving you wondering where I was. If I had a number, I could call if this happened again."

Beth's heart went pitter-pat. He didn't sound like a man just passing the time with her. "Millie's Elden has a cell phone we can use, but it's only supposed to be for emergencies. Jane is pushing Eleanor to get one. Ellie's not keen on it but she says if we get one, it stays off in a kitchen drawer."

He adjusted his straw hat. He had exchanged the dirty, ratty-brimmed one she had seen him wearing that morning for his newer going-to-town hat. "I get it," he said. "My *mam* bought a cell phone a couple of years ago when a cousin in Indiana had a heart attack. The son had to drive seven miles in a buggy to make a call. The cousin didn't make it. Only fifty-five years old. Still my *mam* keeps her cell in the henhouse."

"The henhouse?" Beth chuckled. She could imagine Maree Lehman hiding a phone in a nesting box in her chicken coop, probably so her husband wouldn't realize she had one. Jack's father, Sharar, believed in the old ways established when their people came to America in the eighteenth century. He had little tolerance for modern amenities. His family didn't even have a washing machine run by propane like every other household in Honeycomb. Maree still washed her family's clothes by hand using a wringer.

"*Mam* hides the phone there so no one knows

she has it," Jack continued. "Of course, my brothers and sisters all know it's there, and I suspect some of my brothers have, unbeknownst to her, used it. I have a cell phone because of work." He patted his pocket. "But I asked for permission first, and Bishop Cyrus gave his blessing. I don't make personal calls on it. I only use it to call contractors or the lumbers stores. And to talk to English clients." He lowered his voice until she felt like they were the only two there. "For you, I'd make an exception, though, and risk your uncle's reprimand."

"I'm glad Uncle Cyrus said you could have the phone. Sometimes, he can be cranky, but he's always been a reasonable man." She gazed up at him. She was happy that he had come for her and still wanted to spend time with her. "I'm ready to go if you are. Millie and Cora can take Jane home."

He lifted his chin in the direction of the circle of girls whispering among themselves while taking turns glancing in Jack and Beth's direction. "You don't want to stay and talk to your friends?"

And listen to them talk about you? she thought. *No thank you.* "*Nay*, I'm ready to go," she repeated. "I'll let Millie know and meet you at the wagon."

As she spoke, she realized he was staring at her.

"What?" she asked feeling self-conscious. She wiped the corners of her mouth. "Do I have chocolate frosting on my face? We had iced brownies for dessert."

His smile became tender. "*Nay.* I'm just glad I made it here. It took a while to reattach the horseshoe, then my *dat* wanted me to stay home. And my mother was fussing with me because my *dat* was upset and—" He took a breath and exhaled. "And honestly it would have been easier to stay put, but I'm glad I didn't, because none of that matters now." He reached out and took her hand as he gazed into her eyes. "Because now I'm here with you. Where I want to be."

Beth's breath caught in her throat. His touch made her feel all warm and soft inside. And safe. Safe from what she didn't know, but it was a feeling she'd never experienced before. "I'll be there directly," she told him, and then she made herself pull her hand from his and walk away.

Ten minutes later, Beth had said her good-byes and thank-yous and sat on the wagon seat next to Jack.

"Ready?" he asked, releasing the hand brake.

She clasped her hands on her lap, both excited and relieved to be alone with Jack. All those gossiping women made her nervous. They made her question her judgment of who Jack was. But when she was alone with him, she was confident of her appraisal.

"Other than the horse throwing a shoe, how was your day?" Beth asked as they rode down the lane. The family ran a retail and commercial orchard and both sides of the driveway were lined with trees; there were apples on one side, and peach on the other. Even though the fruit growing on the branches was still tiny, she could smell a sweetness in the air that made her smile.

"It was fine. You know, it was work. We got the last window in on the first floor right before quitting." He glanced at her. "You know me. I could talk all day about my work, but I'd rather hear about your day."

"*Nay*, you wouldn't. Mine was dull. I spent hours transplanting tomato and pepper seedlings from the hothouse to the garden. Then I mucked out the henhouse to use the manure for fertilizer." She flashed him a saucy grin. "Would you like to hear about how many wheelbarrows of manure I hauled?"

He laughed. "Okay, maybe I *don't* want

to hear the details." He held her gaze. "But I want to know how you are, Beth. I barely saw you for five minutes this morning when you checked up on me."

"I was not checking up on you."

He gave her a look that made her laugh.

"*Oll recht*, maybe I was checking up on you just a little."

They both chuckled and he said, "You know, I think about you all the time when we're apart. I miss you."

His words made her feel warm and tingly, and she didn't know how to respond. She'd never gotten close enough to a young man to hear such things. She'd never wanted to hear them from anyone. Until Jack.

She glanced at him and then away, not sure how to respond to his words and the feelings they generated. "Have you been able to find another man for your crew?" she asked, changing the conversation. "You said a roofer you've used has been looking for a general construction job."

He pulled back on the reins when they reached the paved road. "*Ya*, Jethro Kline. Nice guy." He looked one way and then the other before making a left turn. He drove in the opposite direction of her house as he had on other nights from neighbors' homes without asking. Otherwise, she'd be home in less than half an hour, even if he kept the gelding to a walk. "He's a hard worker and willing to take less pay per hour than he's been making as a roofer with the understanding that he'll be apprenticing with me. I'd love to hire him."

"*But*?" she said.

"But, he lives in Rose Valley near Byler's Store. He doesn't have his own horse and buggy so I'd have to fetch him. I don't have time to drive all the way there from my place, then to yours, then take him home at the end of the day. I've got chores to do for my *dat* after the workday. And right now, I'm building your store here in Honeycomb. What if I get a contract farther away?" He stared straight ahead, his tone changing. "What if my *dat*'s right?" he worried aloud. "What if an Amish man can't be a general contractor? What if I can't?"

"I know he's your father and we must respect our elders, but he's wrong, Jack." She daringly reached over and rested her hand over his on the wagon seat. She only did it for a moment and then withdrew.

"That's what I keep telling myself," Jack said. "My *vadder* may know a lot, but he doesn't know everything. He doesn't know *me*." He was quiet for a moment. "Anyway, that's where I am now. The job would go faster with more help, but I haven't found anyone close enough for me to hire."

Beth listened to the rhythmic clip-clop of the horse's hooves and thought about Jack's problem. She knew he was under pressure from his father to be successful quickly, and she wanted to help. "Do you think you could ask Mark to pick up Jethro and take him home at day's end? Maybe pay Mark for the gas?"

Jack shifted the leathers in his hands, considering her suggestion. "Maybe. I'd have to pay for his time traveling to and from. And it would lengthen his workday so I don't know how he would feel about that. As you know, he lives with his sister. He's got chores to do at his house before supper, too."

"Just an idea," Beth said. She studied the country road ahead of them. Honeycomb was situated with no significant roads, so it was quiet and automobile traffic was light. Far in the distance, she saw the taillights of a pickup truck, but there wasn't another car in sight.

"I'll have to think on that," Jack said. "The idea's got potential. *Danki*. My bigger problem right now, though, is getting supplies. I can have the big lumber orders delivered, but

I'm wasting too much time running to the store for this and that. I try to plan days, but there's always one problem or another. The other day I was short on nails for the nail gun. I went for more and then had to turn around and go back to the store because we needed more flashing to finish up the last two windows." He pressed his hand to his forehead. "This is exactly why my *dat* said I'd never be successful as a contractor. You need a truck." He cut his eyes at her. The sun was setting over the treetops to the west, bathing him in a golden light. "And while your uncle, the bishop, might allow a cell phone, I don't think he will allow me to have a pickup. Can you imagine him catching me in a truck on the road and coming after me in his buggy?"

Beth laughed. "I don't think he'd chase you. I think he'd lie in wait to pounce at the jobsite."

"Good point." He laughed with her. "Anyway, I've got to come up with a way to be more efficient. I thought I had everything planned out when I borrowed money from my grandfather to get started, but things have come up that I hadn't anticipated."

"You didn't think this would be easy, did you?"

He looked at her, a half smile on his face. "That's it? That's your encouragement?"

She laughed. "You know what I mean. You must have realized how hard it would be to make your dream come true. But it *is* coming true, one day at a time. I know I don't know much about construction, but you're doing a wonderful job. Nothing slipshod about your work. Everything looks neat and secure."

"*Danki*." He flashed a smile. "That means a lot to me, coming from you. I still talk to my old boss, and when I have a question or hit a problem I'm not sure how to deal with, he's happy to share his knowledge." He tapped his pocket. "Another reason to have the cell phone."

They rode side by side in comfortable silence for a quarter of a mile before Jack asked, "So anything going on next weekend? Bertie Mast's barn raising?"

"*Nay*. Postponed. It was supposed to be next Saturday, but the trusses he ordered haven't arrived. And the following weekend he and his family are attending a wedding in Indiana and will be gone for at least ten days. Henry said she thinks the plan is for mid to late June. Why do you ask?"

"Just wondering when we can have a date."

She looked at him, quizzically. "We're having a date now."

"I mean a real date." He slid his hand across the wooden bench seat and covered hers. "I could take you out to lunch, or…or maybe I could come over some night after supper and we could take a romantic walk in the moonlight." He squeezed her hand. "What do you think, *liebchen*?"

She wasn't sure what she thought. She couldn't think with his hand still on hers and him using such endearments. Thankfully, she didn't have to because she spotted something in the middle of the road not far ahead of them. It took a moment for her to realize what it was, and she grabbed his arm. "Stop!" she cried. "Stop! Don't hit it!"

He pulled hard on the reins. "Don't hit what?"

"The box turtle!" The wagon had barely rolled to a stop when Beth raised the skirt of her dress and jumped down from the wagon. Hearing a car approach, she ran toward it, waving her arms. "*Nay*," she cried, spotting a big red pickup with loud muffler coming toward them at a high rate of speed.

Behind her she heard pounding footsteps. Jack.

"I'll get it. Get off the road!" he shouted. "I recognize that truck. The driver's dangerous."

For a split second, Beth wondered if she could trust Jack. Would he rescue the turtle or back off if the driver didn't slow down? Jack had time to get to it, but none to spare. She took a leap of faith and cut hard toward the shoulder of the road. From a patch of dandelions, she watched Jack grab the turtle as it reached the center line, right in the path of the pickup bearing down on them.

"Jack!" she screamed. "He's not slowing down!"

Jack swerved right and raced toward her. As the truck whizzed by, he stopped right in front of her, panting. Before she could catch herself, she threw her arms around him. Jack wrapped one arm around her shoulder, still holding the turtle with his other hand.

"It's okay," he murmured, pulling her against him. "No harm done. See. It's fine." He held the turtle up to show her that its head was out, its clawed feet pedaling as if it were still crossing the road.

Beth pressed her face into his shoulder. "You could have both been killed." She looked up at him, teary-eyed. "You could have been killed trying to save it. I can't believe you'd risk being hit by a truck for a turtle!"

He smiled. "So, see? All those terrible things folks say about me can't be true, right?"

"I don't know what you mean," she said, easing back, but still not ready to let go of him.

He looked down at her, unruffled. "I think you do. I know there's plenty of gossip about me. But the things they say aren't true. The monster they describe couldn't possibly be the man who saves turtles, could he?"

Beth gazed into his green eyes, and she was afraid he would kiss her for a moment. She was worried she would let him.

"Give it to me," she said, stepping back from him and holding out her hand. "I'll let it go in the woods. Across the road, in the direction it was headed."

He handed her the box turtle and took her hand. "Come on. We'll go together."

Chapter Ten

Beth slid the second pan of chocolate chocolate-chip muffins into Rosie's oven and spun the dial on the plastic timer her friend kept on the counter. "I'll rotate the pans in twelve minutes so the tops cook evenly."

Rosie was making eight dozen muffins for a fundraiser at the Mennonite church she attended, and Beth had offered to help. This way they could spend time together. She hadn't seen Rosie for more than five minutes since she and Jack had begun dating. Beth was too busy getting the garden started, doing her regular chores, overseeing the store's building and making time for her new beau.

She had a boyfriend!

Beth still found it hard to believe that she was walking out with a young man. And it was

Jack Lehman, one of the most sought-after single men in the county. Jack had made it official when he'd introduced her as his girlfriend to an Englisher he'd once worked with. Beth and Jack had been in a fast-food place, eating chicken sandwiches and waffle fries when the man had approached their table. Jack had seemed eager to introduce her and the pride she'd heard in his voice when he'd called her his girlfriend had made her heart flutter.

"What's next?" Beth asked Rosie as she wiped her hands on her apron. She had dropped her father off with Jack at the store at seven that morning and planned to pick him up at one. Jack had offered to walk him home, but Beth knew her father wouldn't like that. Instead, she had packed him a lunch so he could eat with the other men, and she would get him home in time for him to rest before supper. "Do you want to make the apple crumb first or the lemon poppy?"

Rosie was at the sink, washing a mixing bowl. "I don't care. I'm just so happy to see you and be able to catch up on all your news."

"And your news," Beth said, smiling. They'd spent half an hour talking about a young man Rosie's age who had just joined her church and had been making a point to speak with her whenever he had the opportunity. Rosie wasn't certain she was ready to date again, but she knew it was time after being widowed for two years. Alan seemed to be the perfect person to encourage Rosie to dip her toes into the dating waters again.

Rosie's cheeks turned pink. "I don't want to talk about Alan anymore. It makes it too real." She dried off the clean bowl, appearing flustered. "Let's talk about something else."

"Okay, we can talk about something else, but you still need to decide what you're going to do if Alan asks you out for coffee or something. Because he's going to."

"I know, I know." Rosie flapped her hands. "I'm terrified and excited at the same time. Let's make the lemon ones next."

"Lemon poppy seed it is." Beth grabbed a fat, yellow lemon from a wooden bowl in the center of the kitchen table.

"Recipe's there on the counter. I'll get the zester." Rosie began to open cabinet drawers one after the other. "Now where did I put that?" she wondered aloud. She'd told Beth that she had been so bored at home the previous week that she had reorganized her entire kitchen and now she couldn't find a thing. "Oh, I know what I wanted to ask you. What's going on with Cora applying for the school-teacher's job?"

"*Ach*," Beth sighed as she tapped her foot to a country song playing on the radio on the windowsill over the sink. Her uncle, the bishop, would never allow a family in his district to have a radio, but it wasn't explicitly prohibited for his congregants to listen to someone else's radio. As long as the content wasn't inappropriate. "No news on the job yet," she told Rosie. "Jack talked to his brother, and the school board is absolutely interested in interviewing Cora. He got the impression that the women of Honeycomb have been making noises about not having enough women teachers." She waved her hand. "Anyway, apparently the interviews are on hold now until the board members can evaluate the needs of our growing community. They're not sure if we need to build a new Amish school to open in the fall or add an addition to one of the other schools. Jack said his brother mentioned there was talk of looking outside Honeycomb for a new teacher. That has Cora worried, of course. She really, really wants the job."

"Does that mean Eleanor said she could apply?"

Following the recipe, Beth added two cups

of flour to the mixing bowl. "Not yet. But Cora has gotten her to the point where she's agreed to wait on a decision until there are more details about the job."

"What does your father say? Is he okay with one of his daughters working full-time?"

Beth added sugar next. "What does he say on that subject? Nothing. He's all about *his job* these days. He talks nonstop about what his crew has done. I haven't seen him this happy in years." She chuckled. "To hear him talk, you'd think *he* was the contractor and not Jack."

Rosie pressed her lips together but said nothing.

What?" Beth asked as she reached for the baking powder. "Why are you looking at me like that?"

"You know why." Rosie opened another drawer and peered into it. "Aha! Here it is." She held up the zester.

"No, I don't know why." Beth added a pinch of salt to the bowl and glanced down at the recipe again to ensure she'd added all the necessary dry ingredients before mixing them up.

Rosie set the zester on the counter and leaned against it, crossing her arms. She was wearing a pretty chintz-print apron over her modest dress. On her feet, she sported white

Nike sneakers. "You sure you want to talk about this?"

"About what?" Beth asked, although she knew very well what her friend was referring to. Jack. Beth was giving herself a moment before they dove into this conversation again. It wasn't that she didn't want Rosie's opinion, it was just that she desperately wanted her to like Jack. But that didn't mean she wasn't willing to listen to her friend.

"I told you weeks ago that I thought you could do so much better than Jack Lehman," Rosie said, her voice filled with concern. "He's going to break your heart, the same way he broke Willa's. And other girls' hearts, too. I don't mean this to be critical, but you're such an innocent, Beth. You don't know what men can be like. If Jack cheated on Willa, he'll cheat on you." She held up her hands. "I know, I know, you think that no man in the Amish church could be anything but good and kind and faithful, but—"

"I never said that," Beth disagreed.

Rosie pressed her lips together, hesitated and then went on. "I never told you this because—" she looked down at her sneakers "—because it's not right to speak badly of the dead." She gave a laugh that was without humor. "And it's certainly not right to speak badly of a dead husband." She looked up, her face a mask of sadness. "But I know what kind of man Jack is because I was married to one."

Beth stopped stirring the ingredients in the bowl and looked up. "What do you mean?"

"Ralph was unfaithful to me with another woman." Tears filled Rosie's eyes. "With many other women."

"Oh, Rosie," Beth murmured, her heart aching for her friend. "I had no idea. I'm so sorry."

"I'm sorry, too. And you didn't know because I saw no reason to talk to anyone about it." Rosie patted her eyes with the corner of her apron. "I'm not telling you this because I want you to feel sorry for me. God has a reason for everything that happens to us, and even though I don't understand why I was meant to marry Ralph and then lose him, I accept it." She exhaled and looked up at Beth. "My point is that I have experience with men like Jack. And I don't want to see you hurt the way I was."

Beth began mixing the wet ingredients for the lemon muffins, taking her time before she spoke again. She understood why Rosie had a bad opinion of Jack, but she didn't know him. Not like Beth did. "Jack's not going to cheat on me. He cares for me and I care for him."

Beth thought about him walking her back to the house when he got off work the previous day. He had held her hand as they strolled in silence, enjoying the warmth of the day and the closeness to each other. The five-minute walk had made her wish he didn't have to go home. That she didn't. That their home was together. She realized then that she was falling in love with him.

"Rosie," she said, "I found out that Willa's explanation of what happened between her and Jack wasn't exactly what happened."

"What *he* says happened, maybe." The timer went off and Rosie opened the oven, turned the muffin pan and closed the door again.

Beth looked at her friend but didn't speak. It hurt her to hear the animosity in her friend's voice because she cared for Rosie deeply. But she also cared for Jack.

"Fine," Rosie said impatiently. "So, what does Jack say happened?"

Beth exhaled and repeated what Jack had told her about what had passed between him and her sister. As she explained, she was careful not to accuse Willa of telling untruths. Knowing Willa, and now knowing Jack, she understood how there could have been confusion between them. They communicated in different ways and Willa could be impulsive. She didn't always mean what she said in the heat of an argument and sometimes she expected people to know what she was thinking without telling them.

Rosie listened to Beth's explanation as she juiced and zested the lemon. She asked several questions, but it was apparent she would take Willa's side. And when Beth was done, Rosie said, "Well, that's creative. I'll give him that."

Beth let out a groan of frustration. "Rosie, I know Jack. We've talked for hours and hours and he's a good, faithful man. He didn't cheat on Willa and he's not going to cheat on me. When would he have time?" she joked, lightening up the conversation because she didn't want to quarrel with her friend. "He's either on the jobsite at our store, working on his father's farm, or out with me." She waved a measuring cup. "I know where he is and what he's doing every hour of the day. He couldn't sneak off to see Barbara Troyer or anyone else without me knowing."

"Fine," Rosie said. "But my concern is not just about Jack being a player. I didn't want to have to tell you this, but..."

Beth frowned when her friend hesitated. What other secrets could she possibly have?

Beth still hadn't processed that Rosie's deceased husband had been unfaithful to her. "But what?"

When Rosie didn't say anything, Beth urged, "Come on. You can't start a conversation like that and not finish it." She set down the spoon and walked over to Rosie. "Tell me."

Rosie glanced out the windows framed in gingham curtains. The smell of roses drifted in. "Beth," she said, not looking at her, "Jack's the kind of man only out for his own gain, and he's willing to take advantage of others to do so."

Beth went back to mixing up the muffin batter, adding the liquid ingredients to the dry. "What's that supposed to mean?"

"He's buying land."

"I know that. He wants to build spec houses. I think he even talked to my *dat* about buying a couple of acres of road front from him. He wants to buy lots, build affordable homes and sell them. English building contractors do it all the time."

"Do English contractors take advantage of women recently widowed, buying land below value so they can reap more rewards?"

Beth returned to stirring the batter, taking her frustration out on the muffin mix. "What are you talking about? He bought what land?"

"He bought three acres from a Mennonite widow, Betty Grogg. She goes to our church. Her son said Jack Lehman swindled her. That he took advantage of his father's death and offered a pittance, and Betty took it because she needed the money."

Beth shook her head, stirring harder. "Jack wouldn't do that."

"Easy there." Rosie took the wooden spoon from Beth's hand. "You're going to make the muffins tougher than a shoe. The batter isn't supposed to be beaten, just stirred to mix the wet with the dry." She began filling a muffin pan. "Beth, I'm not telling you these things to hurt you. I'm worried about you, about you getting involved with a man like my husband."

Beth turned to her, trying not to be angry. She believed Rosie when her friend said she was telling her these terrible things because she cared about her. "If Jack was—"

The phone on the wall rang, drowning out Beth's voice.

Rosie crossed the kitchen and picked up the receiver. "Hello?" She listened and then said, "She's here. Just a minute." She met Beth's gaze and held out the phone as if it had germs. "For you."

Beth frowned. "For me?"

"Jack," she said, clearly not approving. "I'll be back in a minute."

Why would Jack be calling her at Rosie's? Beth waited until her friend went down the hallway before she put the receiver to her ear. "Jack?"

"Beth." He sounded out of breath, his voice strained. In the background, she heard the wail of a siren. "There's been an accident."

Beth suddenly felt so light-headed that she rested her free hand on the chair rail on the wall for support. "My *dat*?" she asked, her voice wavering. How would she ever forgive herself? If he were hurt on the job—or worse—it would be her fault because she was the one who had gotten Eleanor to agree to let their father work with Jack in the first place.

"*Nay*, not your *dat*," Jack said tenderly. "He's fine, *liebchen*. It's Mark."

Her relief was fleeting and she was short of breath again. She pressed her hand to her chest as she looked down the hall. Rosie had gone to the bathroom and would be back momentarily. She turned around so her friend wouldn't overhear the conversation. "*Ach, nay*," she murmured. "Is it bad?"

"I don't think so. I mean, bad enough, but I think he'll be fine. Pray he will be. He never lost consciousness and talked to me the whole time we waited for the paramedics. He kept apologizing for ending the workday early. But he had to be taken to the hospital. The ambulance just left. Lemuel and I are headed into town in the wagon. Can you tell Rosie what happened and get her to the hospital?"

"Exactly what did happen?" Beth asked, gripping the phone tightly.

"He fell from a ladder. It was an accident. I don't even know how it happened. Your *dat* and I were loading up the nail guns and I heard Mark holler and the crash of an aluminum ladder and then Lem calling for me."

Beth took a deep breath. "But it's not bad?"

"Bad enough to go to the hospital. Looked like a compound fracture of his arm. I don't know what else. But his life's not in danger. Like I said, he was alert and breathing fine. Can you find a way to meet me at the hospital with Rosie? Mark's worried about her and doesn't want her driving herself. He wanted you to make sure that she understood right away that he would be fine. I guess her husband died in an accident, but whoever called her from the hospital didn't tell her he was bad off. Mark said his sister went to the hospital thinking her husband would be okay. And he wasn't."

Beth's thoughts flew in a hundred directions and she had to focus forcibly. "*Ya*, we'll be there as soon as possible," she told Jack with a nod. "I'll call a driver, leave our buggy here and come back for it later. You're sure my *dat*'s *oll recht*?"

"He's right as rain. Henry was working on your fence and heard the ambulance. She ran down and took your *dat* back to the house. Boy, he was angry. He wanted to ride in the ambulance with Mark." Jack said something to someone else, his voice muffled, and then to her, "I've gotta go. Lem's pulled the wagon around. See you at the hospital?"

Beth heard the bathroom door open. "*Ya*, see you there." She hung up and turned to her friend. "Rosie, Mark fell off a ladder at work."

Rosie gasped, covering her mouth with her hand.

Beth rushed to hug her. "He's fine. Jack says he's going to be fine. But he broke his arm." She decided not to give Rosie any further details. If Mark was talking, he really was going to be fine. There was no need for Beth to tell her what Jack had said about the compound fracture. It would be better to get a diagnosis from a doctor, once her brother was seen. "Mark wants you to meet him at the hospital. We're going to go together."

"But he's okay. He's okay," Rosie repeated, struggling to catch her breath.

"He's going to be fine. Just a broken arm." She hugged Rosie and then walked back to the phone. "I'm going to call a driver. We'll be there in no time."

Chapter Eleven

As Jack had suspected, Mark's injury wasn't simply a broken arm. Beth had brought Rosie to the hospital and Rosie had gone in to see her brother in the emergency department. Then Mark was to be taken to an operating room to have his arm set with a steel plate and screws. But, because of a multicar accident, his surgery ended up being postponed until after 7:00 p.m.

At ten thirty that night, Jack sat with Beth in the surgical lounge, waiting for word that Mark had been transported from the recovery to his room for inpatient care.

Rosie and Mark's parents had joined them at the hospital, then had gone home after they saw their son in the recovery room. They took their daughter home with them to stay the night.

After the surgeon had given an update on

Mark's condition in the waiting room—that the surgery had gone well—she had suggested that they all go home and come back to see Mark in the morning . Mark's parents had done as the doctor suggested, but Jack couldn't leave until he knew Mark would be okay. He needed to see his friend and employee with his own eyes.

When Beth had stubbornly refused to leave until he did, Jack was touched. He would have done the same if the roles had been reversed. While they waited, Beth got them food from the cafeteria and arranged for a hired driver to take them home when they were ready to leave. Lemuel had taken their horse and wagon home hours ago.

Jack looked down at Beth, sleeping, her head resting on his shoulder. He smiled. He had a nearly uncontrollable urge to brush her cheek with his fingertips. He wanted to kiss her temple. But he did none of those things because Beth had made it very clear that it was important to her that she follow their community's rules of appropriate behavior for a single woman, and he respected that. So instead of touching her, he watched her, thinking about how much he loved the feeling of her next to him. She smelled so good. Like…lemon cookies.

Today had been a terrible day, but having

Beth with him and supporting him had made it bearable. Because of Beth, Jack had found confidence in himself. As Beth had pointed out, the accident wasn't his fault and he didn't have to feel bad about it. It was just…an accident. It was a concept that was hard for him to wrap his head around because he had been raised to believe that anything wrong that happened was his fault. According to his *dat*, anything that ever went wrong was due to Jack's stupidity, poor performance and even his sins. And while now, as an adult, Jack could rationalize that those things weren't true, it was still hard not to believe them sometimes because his father had been saying cruel things to him for twenty-three years.

Beth's reassuring words had allowed Jack to let go of his guilt to focus on Mark. While Rosie had gone into the room to see her brother, Beth had suggested that she and Jack pray. They had held hands as they prayed together silently, and when he opened his eyes and saw her, a calmness settled over him. The way she looked at him made him feel *Gott*'s love and realize that he loved her.

He had fallen in love with her. When it had happened, or why, he didn't know. The question was, what to do with his feelings. He knew

Beth liked him, but did she love him? Could she love him? Could he ever be enough for her?

Jack knew his father loved him, but nothing Jack ever did was good or right enough. Even now that he was finding success in his chosen line of work, his father constantly criticized him. His father insisted he couldn't make enough money building additions for people. That Jack had to buy land and build houses and sell them. That was where the real money was, his *dat* had said. Jack could see his point, but his parent's pushing made him uncomfortable.

Beth woke and gazed up at him, her face soft and relaxed from sleep.

"You *oll recht*?" she asked softly as she squeezed his hand.

He nodded, emotion welling up in his chest until he couldn't find his voice.

"*Goot*. Because you heard the doctor. Mark is going to be fine. The broken arm was his only injury. Impressive from an eighteen-foot fall. The doctor said Mark was lucky," she went on, "but you and I know there's no such thing as luck. It was *Gott* protecting him. That's why it wasn't worse."

"*Ya*, but the doctor said that his recovery will take time." Anxiety began to creep in and Jack slipped his hand from Beth's. He leaned forward, clasping both sides of his head, and propped his elbows on his knees. Now that his fear of Mark having life-threatening injuries had passed, Jack had other things to worry about. Like his fledgling construction company. "Mark won't be climbing a ladder for months. And I'm going to have to pay him while he's recovering. My crew is my responsibility."

"But you don't know that it will be months," she said.

"The doctor said months. He also said that Mark might need another surgery."

"But only if the healing doesn't go as the doctor hopes it will," Beth said. "He's young and healthy. He's going to heal just fine."

Jack continued to hold his head in his hands, surprised by how quickly he could slide back into self-deprecation. What if his father was right? What if he couldn't be a contractor? "And if I pay Mark without him working for me, how will I hire another worker? I'm already shorthanded." He glanced at her. "I'm not even sure I'm going to be able to finish the store. My *vadder* was right. I should have stuck to farming."

"Nonsense," Beth said. She wore a lavender dress and white apron with an organza prayer *kapp*. Though she was as tired as he was, she was as pretty as ever. "You're going to finish it because you have to."

He groaned and leaned back in the chair, tucking his hands behind his head. They'd been sitting there for so long that he needed to get up and stretch his legs, but he didn't know if he had the energy.

"Let's think about this. Take things one step at a time. First Mark, then the next problem." She was quiet and then spun in the chair to face him. "Will he be able to drive?"

Jack had just closed his eyes. "What?" He opened them.

"Will Mark be able to drive? The doctor said something about restrictions, but..."

He could almost see the wheels of her mind turning.

"But I think the doctor said no driving for a week," she continued. "No driving if he was taking any pain medication, but... What about after the ten days?"

"I'm not following." Jack glanced at the clock on the wall. It was now 10:50 p.m. He wondered if he should call the driver Beth had arranged to take them home. He could return tomorrow to see Mark, as the surgeon had suggested.

"In ten days, Mark should be able to drive again. He's right-handed and his left arm is what's broken. And his truck is automatic." She opened her arms wide. "Mark can drive for you."

Jack frowned. She wasn't making any sense. "Drive where?"

"Wherever you need him to. To transport another man to and from the jobsite."

"I told you, Beth. I don't have the cash to pay another worker."

"When you were talking about the roofer, you seemed to think you could pay someone else."

"Beth—"

"*Nay*, hear me out." She clasped his wrist. "Hire Mark to be a driver. He can pick you and Lem up in the morning to get there faster. And he can pick up the new guy."

"What new guy?"

"The roofer." She snapped her fingers. "Jacob Kline, Jason Kline? What was his name?"

"Jethro Kline," Jack said.

"*Ya*, and while you wait until Mark is healed enough to drive, you can build that shed for the lady who accepted the quote from you. The one who saw your card pinned to the bulletin board at Byler's. By the time you get back to our store, you'll have some money from that job and you can hire Jethro. And you'll have Mark driving for you." She held up a finger. "And not just to get your crew to and from our store. You can have him run back and forth to the lumber stores for you. You've said that you're wasting hours driving back and forth in a horse and wagon some days. Mark has a big trailer he can pull behind his truck. I've seen it in Rosie's barnyard. He'll get lumber when you need it, so you don't have to depend on deliveries."

Jack watched her, thinking she might be on to something. "*Oll recht,*" he said drawing out the words. "But even if I can make the money work to pay Mark as a driver and hire Jethro, if Mark is out two weeks, I'm behind on the store build by two weeks. I promised your family it would be done by August."

"Hmm," she said, thoughtfully tapping her chin with her finger.

They both looked up as a male nurse in scrubs stepped into the waiting room. "Mrs. Dorn?" he called, looking around the small space that smelled of coffee.

Jack and Beth were the only two in the waiting room. Jack shook his head. "Sorry. But we were waiting to hear if Mark Berger had been taken to his room. Someone was supposed to let us know."

The nurse held up his hand. "I need to find Mrs. Dorn and let her know how her husband's doing, and then I'll check on your friend."

"Thank you," Jack said. When the man was gone, he looked at Beth. "So back to your plan. I hire Mark to drive, get Jethro to work for me. That makes sense. But I don't know if the three of us—and your *dat* can finish the store on time."

She tucked a lock of hair that had fallen from her *kapp* behind her ears. "Henry," she declared, obviously pleased with herself.

He ran his hand over his face and felt beard stubble. It had been such a long day and he was so tired, mentally and physically. "Henry who?"

"Henry my sister. *Henrietta.*" Beth rose from her chair and placed it in front of him. "Henry would love to work with you to finish the store."

"You want me to hire *Henry*?" he asked. He was so exhausted that he wondered if he was hearing things. "A woman?"

Her gaze narrowed and she planted her hands on her hips. "You're not hiring her. She'll help with our building," she said, her tone becoming terse. "*Ach,* Jack, please don't tell me you wouldn't want her to work with you for free because she's a woman."

When he saw the fire in Beth's eyes, Jack realized he'd almost made a terrible mistake. The thought had crossed his mind, but it was spurred more by what others might think, like his father, than his own beliefs.

"You don't think she can do it? She fixes everything at our place. She patches roofs, builds laying boxes and hangs doors. She replastered a wall over the winter and she's very good at painting walls and trim. She might not know a lot about rough construction, but that stuff's all done. She really could help you, Jack. And I think you should let her."

He rose from the chair. "You're right."

She drew back in surprise. "I am?"

He grinned. "It's a brilliant idea." He tipped his head to one side and then the other, stretching, thinking. What would other people in their community say? Their bishop? And he didn't want to consider what his father's response would be. But Beth's plan could work.

"Do you think Henry will agree?" He stood in front of Beth. "More importantly, will Eleanor let her?"

Beth laughed. "You don't know Henry very

well. No one *lets* Henry do anything. She does what she pleases."

Jack stroked his chin. "You know, it sounds like a crazy plan, but it might work, Beth." He took a step closer as he gazed into her blue eyes. As he looked at her, he wondered what it would be like to wake up to those beautiful eyes every morning. To the determination he saw on her face. With a woman like Beth at his side, he knew he could be successful in his business. More importantly, he knew he could be the man he wanted to be.

The male nurse stepped back into the waiting room. "Mrs. Dorn is still MIA," he said. "But I found your Mr. Berger. If you'll follow me, I'll point you in the right direction. It's late for visitors, but I checked with the charge nurse and you can see him for a few minutes."

Jack looked at Beth again. "Want to come with me?" He offered his hand to her.

She smiled, taking it. "Of course."

Together they rode the elevator to the third floor to check on Mark. As the elevator rose, Jack thought about his feelings for Beth, which grew stronger with every new day.

Was this love? he wondered. And if it was, what was he going to do about it?

Chapter Twelve

Standing under the shade of a broadleaf oak tree on Bert Mast's property, Beth made eye contact with Jack as he walked past her. He and his older brother carried ten-foot-long two-by-fours toward the two-story gambrel roof that had taken shape over the day. Beth and Jack didn't speak to each other. They didn't have to. Their eyes communicated their feelings. Just seeing him made her eager for the workday to be over so they could spend an hour or so alone together before they returned to their families.

The day had been long but delightful, and Beth couldn't remember when she'd last enjoyed a barn raising so much. Leaning back against the sturdy trunk of the oak, she slipped off her navy canvas sneakers and wiggled her bare feet in sweet-smelling clover. Though it was June and could have been quite hot, the Bert Mast family had been blessed with fair weather for the vast undertaking that involved fifty men and boys and an equal number of women and girls to support them. After losing his barn to a fire in a thunderstorm the previous fall, the barn raising had been a long time coming, and there was an air of excitement in the family and all of Honeycomb.

Beth and her sisters had been busy since sunup, cooking, helping to mind the children and squeezing dozens and dozens of lemons to make lemonade for the workers. It seemed that half the Amish in the county, and several from out of state, had come to help rebuild the large dairy barn, and everyone—from toddlers to white-haired elders—had been hungry. As adult women, a great deal of the heavy work of feeding people fell to them, but Beth didn't mind. She was happy to help the Mast family and be a part of a large community project. Besides, barn raisings were fun. They were a change from everyday chores, which were always welcome, and gatherings like these gave young people from different church districts an opportunity to meet and socialize. Getting to know eligible men was the first step in courtship as the eventual goal of every Amish girl was to find a husband.

Not that Beth was in the market. While she and Jack hadn't discussed their feelings for each other, or marriage, it was on her mind, and she sensed it was on his. She was in no hurry to have that conversation, however. Not yet, at least. Marriage was a lifetime commitment, and she didn't want to rush into such a weighty decision. Beth was sure she was in love with Jack, but was he the man *Gott* intended her to marry? She asked that question each night in prayer but still waited for an answer.

Since they'd begun seeing each other in public, Beth knew there was plenty of talk behind their backs. Despite Willa's continued insistence that she was okay with Beth dating Jack, there were folks in their community who disagreed, and they didn't mind gossiping about it among themselves. Some believed that no young woman in Honeycomb should walk out with a man like Jack Lehman. The kind of man they *thought* he was.

Beth rubbed the back of her neck and stretched. This was the first chance she'd found to take a break in hours and under the cool shade of the oak trees was the perfect place.

Her chosen spot was slightly private, while offering an ideal view of Jack and his brothers framing an interior barn wall was a definite plus. She liked watching him work. He moved with great physical strength and confidence in his abilities. He was a good carpenter; she knew that from watching her family's store rise from a patch of grass to a story and a half building with a roof, windows, siding and the interior walls they'd begin painting on Monday. Of course, being a good carpenter didn't mean that Jack would make a good husband, she reminded herself.

She still vacillated between being certain she knew the man Jack was and worrying about the words of warning she had received about him, especially from Rosie. Rosie's opinion rested heavily on Beth's heart because she knew that her friend had no ulterior motives, unlike some of the jealous girls in Honeycomb. And Rosie had experience with a *player*, as she had called Jack, like her husband had been. Beth was still trying to wrap her mind around the fact that Ralph had been unfaithful. From things Beth had heard from Rosie in the past, her husband had also been rather good-looking, like Jack. He had been highly sought after among the single girls in the Mennonite community and could have had his pick.

Was it a mistake for Beth to trust her instincts? Were her feelings instincts at all, or was she so infatuated with Jack that she didn't see him for who he truly was?

What about what Rosie had said about Jack taking advantage of the Mennonite widow? Could it be true? Beth hadn't brought up the subject with him, but she'd been stewing over it for two weeks. Beth told herself she hadn't talked with him about it because things had been so hectic since Mark's accident. Watching him, she wondered now if she was being truthful with herself. Had she avoided the conversation for fear she would discover that he *had* taken advantage of the widow?

She sighed and leaned against the tree's rough bark, tucking her hands behind her. No matter how hard the conversation would be, she knew she had to talk to Jack about the widow. It was the only way she could move forward with Jack.

"Beth!"

Beth turned around to see Jane heading in her direction "Eleanor said to let you know we're packing up to go," she said. "*Dat*'s tired and he tried to steal one of Edna's newborn kittens. Cora found it in his pocket."

Beth wasn't surprised that their father had tried to take a cat home with him. He had been beside himself since the cat he'd been sneaking into their house had disappeared. It happened with barnyard cats. Sometimes they wandered away, sometimes people picked them up and took them home and sometimes they were carried away by foxes. Of course, they hadn't given their father any of those scenarios. Instead, Jane told him that the cat had gone on an adventure.

"Eleanor wants to know if you're coming home with us or if Jack is bringing you home," Jane said. She took a bite of *apfelstrudel* from a paper plate.

"I'm riding home with Jack." Beth slipped her feet back into her sneakers. It was time to help Edna rett up her kitchen. "I told her that."

"That's what I said." Jane stuffed another big piece of the strudel into her mouth with a plastic fork. "But she said to ask you anyway." She licked her lips while she studied Beth thoughtfully. "Are you going to marry him?"

Her little sister's question took Beth by surprise. "He hasn't asked me."

Jane pointed the fork at Beth. "I mean if he asks you. Henry says she sees how you are together and thinks you're going to get married. But Willa says you're too smart to marry him. I'm not sure which side to take."

Beth started toward the house. "There's no side to take. We don't take sides in our family." She looked down at Jane, who was very petite. "And it's not your business, schweschter. Or theirs," she added. "None of you should be talking about my relationship with Jack. Or any boy. Dating is supposed to be private."

Jane sighed, licking the last of the apfelstrudel from her fork. "I know, but talking about Jack is more fun than talking about how the green bean crop is doing and if the corns on Dat's feet are getting worse." They walked side by side. "I think you should."

"Think I should what?" Beth asked.

"Marry Jack." Jane met her gaze. "I know what some folks are saying about him. That he's not a good man and that he's going to be like his father. But I don't believe it. I see how he looks at you when you don't know he's watching. The man I marry someday, I want him to look at me the same way."

Beth smiled and slid her arm around her sister's shoulder. "Danki."

"For what?" Jane asked. They had made their way to the plastic folding tables, where multiple meals had been served under another copse of oak trees. Thirteen-and four-teen-year-old boys broke down the tables to load them onto a church wagon. As the boys stacked the tables, women and girls wove their way around them, carrying the leftovers into the house to be packed up and passed out for families to take home.

"Thank you for being you," Beth told her sister. "Now, let's load our things so you can get Dat out of here before he tries to stuff one of Edna's goats into his pocket.

Two hours later, as the purple shadows of twilight settled over the Mast farmstead, Beth studied the new barn searching for Jack. Most of the families who'd come to work and visit had already packed up and gone home. Only a few of those who lived nearby remained, and they were busy loading wagons and herding wayward children.

Where was he? Beth wondered. She hadn't seen him in hours. Had he forgotten he was taking her home? Not that it would be far for her to walk home. Their house was only a mile and a half away, less if she cut through the neighbors' properties that intersected with Plum Tree Road. Scanning the area of the barn that was already half covered in clapboard siding that had been rescued from an old outbuilding in Sussex County, she saw no sign of Jack and headed back to the house.

She had almost reached Edna's back door when she spotted him standing next to his family's wagon in the barnyard. Lemuel was on the driver's side of the bench seat with a girl sitting as far from him as possible without falling out of the wagon. The sight made her giggle. She couldn't tell who the girl was from that distance, nor could she hear what Jack was saying, but she suspected he was giving his little brother instructions. It appeared that Lem was taking the young lady home, a first for him.

Beth waited until Lem and the girl rolled out of the barnyard and then called to Jack. When he saw her, he grinned. They met halfway beneath another giant broadleaf oak in the Masts' yard.

"*Hallo*," Beth said, unable to stop smiling. When they were apart, she had so many doubts. She questioned her feelings for him, his honesty in who he seemed to be, she even wondered if Willa was still holding a candle for him. But the moment they made eye contact all that melted away.

His smile for her was equally as significant as hers. "Hello, yourself," he said. "Guess you saw Lem take our transportation."

They stood facing each other, close enough to hold hands, but they didn't. Beth wasn't comfortable with physical displays of affection in front of her friends and family, and Jack respected that. It wasn't the Amish way, although it seemed to her that all Millie and her fiancé, Elden did was hold hands and gaze into each other's eyes.

"*Ya*, I did see him leave," Beth acknowledged.

"I hope it's okay." He slid his hands into his pockets. "I figured it was, but I looked for you to check. Couldn't find you anywhere and Lem was eager to go."

"I was probably in Edna's cellar putting away some canning jars. I made three trips so it would have been easy to miss me."

"I know I should have waited to ask you. You and I already made plans, but Lem had himself turned inside out wanting to ask Maddie Chupp if he could take her home."

Pleasantly surprised, Beth raised her eyebrows. At almost twenty-one, it was time Lem began dating, but he was so shy around girls that Jack had been concerned his little brother would remain a bachelor his whole life. "Maddie Chupp, is it?" Beth asked. The Chupps were new to Honeycomb. Beth didn't know the family well, but they seemed nice.

"*Ya*. When Lem decided to ask her, he got so worked up that I had to find him some antacid tablets."

Beth laughed. "But I guess it went well."

"I guess it did. She looked as nervous as he did when they left, but I told Lem you have to start somewhere. You know what he said to me?"

Beth waited.

"He said girls were scary."

Beth chuckled. "And what did you say?"

He smiled boyishly. "I said *Ya, bruder.* They are."

They grinned at each other and Beth was so happy to be there. To be able to laugh with Jack. They hadn't seen much of each other since Mark's accident. For the last two weeks, Jack and Lem had been building a shed that turned out to be a small garage for the woman who'd found his number on the Byler's store bulletin board. Because Jack's customer lived in Dover, there hadn't been time for Jack to see Beth after work. Not when he needed to get home in time to do the chores expected of him. But the side-job was done, Jack had money in his pocket and on Monday, the plan was for him to work on the store with his new crew: Lemuel, Jethro, her *dat*, and Henry. Beth didn't know who was more excited to get to work, Henry or her father. And Beth was looking forward to seeing Jack every day because she'd missed him terribly.

"Anyway," Jack said. "I thought we could walk to your place. Lem's going to pick me up at your store. I don't imagine he'll be gone too long. From the look on Maddie's face, she may jump out before he rolls to a stop at her door."

Beth smiled. "*Nay*, Lem's going to be fine. I know he's shy, but he can be very charming. Like his brother." She brushed her fingertips across his muscular forearm. The skin-to-skin sensation was brief, but she felt a little shiver every time they touched. "And the walk home sounds perfect." She pressed her hand to her stomach. "I ate too much today. I had two slices of lemon meringue pie and some bread pudding. I need to walk it off."

"Three desserts?" he teased.

"Look who's talking. I saw you eating what looked like a quart of ice cream on top of some sort of pie at the supper break. I couldn't even tell what kind of pie it was, there was so much ice cream."

"I'll have you know it was not pie, it was berry buckle," he told her. "You ready to go?"

She opened her arms. "I am if you are."

"I'm ready. Lem has my tools and my water jug. And I've got a flashlight." He pulled it from his back pocket and held it up. "Do you need to say goodbye to anyone?"

"I already said my goodbyes," she said, eager to be alone with him. "Let's go."

They cut across the Masts' field, and when they were out of sight of anyone who might still be in the yard, Jack took her hand. As they walked, they talked about the day and the work left to be done on the barn. At the edge of the Mast property, they reached Joe Swartzentruber's woods and followed a path that would come out close to her father's property.

As the subject changed from Bert Mast's barn to what Jack needed to do to finish the store, Beth's thoughts drifted to what Rosie had told her weeks ago. With each step through the dark woods, following Jack's flashlight beam, Beth got more upset about what her friend had accused Jack of doing. Beth knew it couldn't be accurate, but what if it was? Things were getting serious with Jack. Even though they hadn't talked about their future together, she sensed it was on his mind as much as it was hers. She could feel it, plus he'd commented a couple of days ago when they'd managed to meet at Byler's for ice cream. He'd joked that someday they would take their children there and he would never let them eat pistachio ice cream like their mother. Beth loved pistachio and bought it every time she went to Byler's. The comment had thrilled and scared her at the same time, because she could imagine taking her children there one day, and she wanted them to be Jack's children.

Once they exited the woods, it was only a hundred yards to the new driveway that led up to the store's new parking lot. By the time they reached it, Beth felt like she would burst. She had to ask Jack about the widow, because she didn't want to dream of taking her and Jack's children for ice cream if she couldn't marry him.

"No sign of Lem yet," Jack said as they reached the dark store. Using the flashlight, he pointed to the front porch with its newly poured cement floor and brick steps. "Do you have to get home or can you sit a minute?"

Beth hesitated. She wanted to go home, stick

her head in the sand and pretend Rosie had never said anything to her.

But she couldn't do that.

"I can stay for a few minutes," she told him. "I... I need to talk to you, anyway."

"Oll recht." He shined the flashlight beam so she could see the steps, and when they were seated side by side, he clicked it off. "Mosquitoes," he told her.

Then he turned to look at her. She couldn't see his eyes in the dark, but she could feel the warmth of his body so close to hers that his pant leg brushed the skirt of her dress.

"What do you want to talk about, *liebchen*."

Beth felt sick to her stomach. She clasped her hands together and turned to him. "About the widow Betty Grogg, Jack."

Chapter Thirteen

"Betty Grogg?" Jack asked, surprised she even knew the woman's name. "How do you know Betty?"

"I don't." Beth didn't look at him.

Jack was confused. They'd had a nice walk together, talking and sharing their day. One of the aspects he treasured most in their relationship was how easily they could talk. When they left the Mast farm, Beth had seemed happy with him. Now suddenly her tone had changed. He could tell he was in trouble. He just didn't know why.

"That's why I want to ask you about her," she added.

"Well, I'm not dating her, if that's what you want to know," he joked. "She's older than my *grossmammi*, Beth."

When Beth didn't laugh, he realized she was upset, and he had no idea why. What had he done? Did he say something wrong?

He didn't think so. What had more likely happened was that while spending the day with so many women, she must have heard another rumor about him. That was the problem with large community events like a barn raising. Yes, good deeds were accomplished, but well-attended gatherings created an opportunity for too much nattering. And not just among the females. Folks talked about women gossiping, but as far as he could tell, men were just as bad.

Jack knew that most of the time when someone passed on *news* of a friend or relative, or even someone they didn't know, it wasn't meant to be harmful. The Amish of Honeycomb lived in an isolated community and their world was small, as they believed *Gott* intended it to be. But with no internet, no music and limited approved reading material, it was human nature that people spent hours every day chatting. And when folks talked, sometimes they told untruths. He didn't believe that people purposely changed facts or made them out of thin air. But everyone knew that when a story was told often enough, it had a way of changing and not always for the good.

What were his friends and neighbors saying about him now?

Fighting irritation, Jack got to his feet. He was tired of people talking about him behind his back. And it seemed to be getting worse. Where could it be coming from?

He glanced at Beth. He considered turning the flashlight back on to see her better, but a three-quarters moon had risen in the dark sky, casting white light over them. "What do you want to know about Betty Grogg?"

"Did you buy land from her?"

He scowled. "Who told you that?"

"Please answer me, Jack. Did you?"

Rather than snapping back at her, he thought about her question for a moment and why it annoyed him.

He didn't mind Beth asking him about his business transactions. If things went the way he had been praying they would, he intended to ask her to marry him once he had some money in the bank again. And he thought she'd say yes. The day Mark had been injured, Jack had talked to Beth's father that morning about wanting to marry her. Jack hadn't directly asked Felty's permission. He didn't think Beth would like that. It would be too old-fashioned for an independent woman like her. And really, it was her decision who she would spend the rest of her life with, not her father's. But Jack wanted to get Felty's feelings on the matter and their conversation had gone well. So once he and Beth were married, she would know every detail of his finances and his business. So, it wasn't the question about his finances that irked him, it was that she was asking because of something someone else told her.

"Well?" Beth asked, rising from the step. "Did you or did you not buy land from Betty Grogg?"

"*Ya*, I did. Right after Epiphany. Enough for two lots where I plan to build homes to sell."

She crossed her arms. "Did you pay her a fair price?"

"What?" he demanded. What was she insinuating?

"You heard me. Did you pay her fair price or pay her less than the land was worth?" She set her jaw. "Jack, I'm asking if you took advantage of the widow because she needed the money after her husband died."

He fought the anger that made his jaw tense. Who was telling her such lies? And why? "Beth, what made you ask such a question?"

She stared at him, arms crossed.

When he realized she wasn't going to say where she had heard the lie, he exhaled, tempering his anger before he spoke. "*Nay*, I did not cheat her out of any money. In fact, I paid more than I should have. According to my *vadder*," he added, trying to keep his bitterness at bay. "*Dat* said I was a fool because I was too generous. That's why my money is so tight right now." He pointed at the nearly completed building behind her. "Until the balance is paid after I finish the store."

"Really, Jack?" she asked, her tone softening.

"You don't have to take my word for it. You can go online at the library and see what I paid if you don't believe me. Probably get the information at the county offices." He shrugged. "It's public information, Beth. How could I lie about something like that? *Why* would I?"

"You didn't do it," she sighed with noticeable relief. "Of course, you didn't," she added softly. "I knew you wouldn't do something like that."

They were both quiet for a moment. As Jack's anger subsided, he removed his straw hat and ran his fingers through his hair. He was tired, not just from the day but from weeks, months of burning the candle at both ends, as his mother liked to say. A man couldn't get ahead if he didn't work hard. But right now, he needed a shower and a good eight hours of sleep.

He looked at her. "Beth, why would you ask me such a thing? What have I said or done that would make you think I could steal from a widow?" He made one hand into a fist at his side. "That I would steal from *anyone*? Who put you up to this? Was it Willa?" He pointed at her. "Because if your sister—"

"It wasn't Willa," she interrupted. She took a step toward him. "I'm sorry I had to ask, Jack. I don't mean to argue, and I didn't mean to hurt you. But I had to be sure of the truth."

He glanced into the darkness, his gaze settling on a neat stack of bricks. There were some days when he wondered if he should have left Honeycomb when he had the opportunity. His grandfather had wanted him to join him in Wisconsin and start his construction business there. Jack had seriously considered it, especially since his grandfather was financing his business. In the end, though, he had decided he couldn't leave his mother. It wasn't easy being married to his father, and it was necessary to Jack that he be there for his mother to act as a buffer between his parents when his *dat* lost his temper. His father had never hit his mother to his knowledge, but Jack had always feared it might come to that.

Jack studied Beth's face in the moonlight and tried not to think about how beautiful she was or how badly his heart would be broken if this relationship ended any way but in marriage. If they were going to make it work, though, they had to be able to talk to each other even when the subject was difficult. So, although a part of him had been annoyed that she would think he would take advantage of someone, he was proud of her because she spoke up. "Anything else you want to ask me?" he said.

She glanced down as if debating whether to say something and then met his gaze again. "*Ya*, one more thing. So we can clear the air before…" She hesitated. "Before we discuss what comes next for us."

Jack's heart swelled and he felt as if he were on a roller coaster like the one he'd ridden at the state fair last summer. Although she hadn't come right out and brought up the subject of marriage, he knew that she was thinking about it.

Beth went on. "I remember when you were walking out with Willa, she mentioned my father possibly selling you some of our land. I remember hearing Willa talk to *Dat* about it, telling him he should sell it to you. That wasn't why you were dating her, was it? To get a good deal with our *dat*?" She chewed on her bottom lip. "Not why you started dating me when Willa broke up with you? Why you told my *dat* he could work for you? All to get on his good side?"

"Are you serious?" Jack asked. This time he wasn't even angry. He was simply…flabbergasted. "*Nay*, Beth, I did not date Willa and I am not walking out with you so I can get in good with your *dat*. I invited him to work with me because he wanted to and it was the right thing to do. There was no other reason." He ran his hand over his face. "Beth, when have I ever given you the impression that I'm that kind of person?"

"You haven't," she whispered, touching his arm. "You understand, don't you? Why I'm asking you about these things. When you hear something so terrible about someone you l— *care for*," she added quickly. "You have to ask, otherwise it…it can fester."

He lifted his gaze and studied her beautiful face in the moonlight, his heart beating faster. Had she almost said she loved him? No girl had ever said that to him before. He'd never wanted anyone to say it. He had hoped and prayed that Beth was falling in love with him, just as he was falling in love with her.

Suddenly he felt as if a weight had been lifted from his shoulders. Beth loved him. It was on the tip of his tongue to blurt that he felt the same way. He wanted to say, "Beth Koffman, I love you and I want to marry you."

But what right did he have to declare his love and ask her to be his wife? He was practically penniless. Everything he had saved since he'd begun working full-time at sixteen years old was invested in his business. And he owed his grandfather money. What did he have to offer Beth right now? Until he finished the store, he had no money. And right now, though he had a couple of bids out, he had no job when the store was completed. Jack had told Felty he wouldn't ask Beth for her hand until he had money in the bank. Money for the materials to build a small house for them, because he would not ask her to sleep under his father's roof as his sister-in-law did. Not for one night. Jack had even brought up buying land from the older man, though for a different purpose than initially. And Felty's response had been kind and generous.

Jack was relieved Beth didn't press him anymore about her father's land.

"I'm sorry I had to ask you those things, Jack," she repeated. "Can you forgive me?" She pressed her hands to her cheeks. The air had grown still and it seemed as if it was warmer out than it had been before sunset. "I don't know what's wrong with me. I second-guess myself too often." She chewed on her lower lip. "I think I'm just tired. And scared," she added.

He reached out and gently caressed her cheek. "Scared of me?"

She shook her head, not meeting his gaze. "Of myself. Of making bad choices."

He smiled, lowering his hand although he didn't want to. "I don't think you could ever make a bad choice, Beth. You're the smartest woman I've ever known." He took a step closer to her, thinking he might try to kiss her. "You're the most beautiful woman I've ever known. Inside and out."

She lifted her lashes to gaze into his eyes.

Suddenly he felt nervous. Should he ask her if he could kiss her? Or just do it?

He'd kissed girls before, but not nearly as many as the women in Honeycomb might say. But somehow, this seemed different. How did a man kiss the woman he wanted to be his wife?

Did he kiss her before their wedding day? Or was it better to wait?

Before Jack could decide, he heard the clip-clop of hooves and turned around to see the lights of a horse and wagon turning off the road and into the new parking lot. It was Lem.

Jack looked back at Beth. "There's my ride. Let me walk you to the house before I go."

"I can walk up my lane on my own, Jack Lehman," she said, but he could tell she was only teasing him.

Her anger was gone. She had believed him when he told her the truth about the widow, and he was so relieved because he didn't know where their relationship could have gone if she didn't believe him. How could a man and a woman commit to a lifetime together if they didn't trust each other?

"I know you can walk by yourself, but I'm not ready to leave you yet," he told her.

Lemuel pulled up close to the porch and Jack looked over his shoulder. His little brother grinned from ear to ear. "Guess things went well with Maddie Chupp," he whispered to Beth.

She gave him a playful push. "Go on with you. Lem looks like he will burst if he doesn't tell you about his evening."

"So, everything is *oll recht*?" Jack motioned to her and then to himself. "Between us?"

She tucked her hands behind her back. "*Ya*. We're fine. See you at Elden's tomorrow for Visiting Sunday?"

He grimaced. "Sorry. I can't. I promised *Mam* I would take her to see an ill friend over in Seven Poplars. She doesn't like to take the buggy so far by herself. And *Dat* doesn't like it anyway."

"He won't go with her?"

"My *dat* doesn't do Visiting Sundays. He stays home and reads the Bible. But don't worry," he added, afraid she might wonder if he would feel the same way when he became the head of their household. "I think every Sunday is important. For different reasons, of course."

"*Guder nummadag*," she told him beaming at him. "I'll see you Monday."

"See you Monday," Jack repeated and got into the wagon with his brother. All the way home, as he listened to Lem talk, Jack thought about Beth and how close he was to becoming her husband.

The following week Beth and Willa went to Spence's Bazaar to drop off two bushels of sweet corn for sale, and Jane tagged along. As they had driven by their store that now looked like a country store, complete with a Coming Soon! sign, Beth caught a glimpse of Jack. She waved to him, and he waved back but then returned to his work on the brick sidewalk he and a mason were putting in.

Beth had been so relieved to have the conversation with him the night of the barn raising. For days after she felt as if she were walking on clouds. She knew it would only be a matter of time until Jack asked her to marry him, and she knew what her answer would be. It would be a hearty yes.

Unfortunately, they hadn't had much time to talk since then. While they had been going on dates regularly while he was putting up the Englisher's outbuilding, he'd be working long hours at the store to finish it up as quickly as possible. With Mark doing all the driving for him, Jack had found that, as Beth suggested, he could get far more work done in a day. The downside was that his hard work took away from their time together. They hadn't even seen each other over the weekend except at church, and then there had only been time for a quick hello and no opportunity for time alone. But Beth knew if she wanted to marry Jack that she would have to learn how to handle the cycles of his job. She knew there would be short days, like in the middle of the winter or the rainy season when he would work fewer hours a week. But there would also be long days when he would leave early in the morning and not return until it was dark, like when daylight hours were their longest. And she knew that she would be the kind of wife who could deal with that. She could handle the animals and the chores when he wasn't home and care for the children, should they be so blessed.

Once Beth and her sisters arrived at Spence's, they carried the bushels of corn to a friend's produce stall, then made their way into the food building. Each had an intention in mind, and they agreed to meet at the buggy in half an hour. Jane wanted to get pink iced donuts to take to a friend's house for a morning sewing session the following day. Beth was headed to a stall to purchase pretzel dogs for her father because they were his favorite. And Willa's sole goal was to flirt with a young man from Lancaster she'd met two weeks ago, who worked in his father's deli. She was supposed to buy ham and cheese, but Jane and Beth had agreed that their sister would probably forget her shopping.

The food and dining annex of the market was packed with people, Englishers and Amish, grabbing late morning coffee and snacks or an early lunch. It was a popular place for single Amish men on work crews to buy lunch. Not only could they get hearty, hot or cold lunches, but they were likely to meet single women from Kent County and from Lancaster County as well. Several food stalls were run by families from Pennsylvania, who hired vans to carry them back and forth to the food market the three days a week that Spence's operated.

When Beth walked up to the pretzel stall, a young woman from Lancaster, Lettie Graber, was wiping down the counter. "Beth," she said with a smile. "I haven't seen you in weeks." As she spoke, she tidied up the condiments on the end of the counter. "I was afraid your *dat* had gone off our pretzel dogs."

Beth laughed. "No fear of that. I've been busy, and it's a bit of a ride into town for us. But we brought sweet corn to sell at a friend's stall. We somehow ended up with double the crop than we usually have this early in July."

"*Ya*, must be something with the weather," Lettie said. "We've more corn than we know what to do with, too. My *mam* has made corn fritters, creamed corn and corn casserole this week. My *dat* keeps teasing her that he wouldn't be surprised if he gets corn in his pancakes."

Beth laughed. "We've already canned enough to last us until next July. I'm not sure what we'll do with it all when the next round ripens."

Seeing that someone had gotten in line behind Beth, Lettie moved to the cash register. "What can I get you, Beth?"

"Excuse me. Excuse me," a woman said, approaching the register. She was tall with red hair that couldn't possibly have been the color God gave her. It looked like the color of a ripe eggplant and Beth had to look away so the woman wouldn't see her trying to suppress a giggle.

"I have a question about your pretzels." She butted in line in front of Beth and the customer behind Beth. "My friend says your products are all gluten and dairy-free, but…"

Beth moved slightly to the side as the woman pushed her way forward, still talking. While she waited as Lettie politely explained that their pretzels were not gluten and dairy-free, her gaze fell on a group of Amish women around twenty years of age. They were standing off to the side, waiting for the next batch of pretzels to come out of the oven. None of them were from Honeycomb, but Beth recognized a pretty, petite girl, who seemed to be the center of attention. She couldn't put a name to the face, however. They were talking and giggling, obviously interested in their conversation.

As the customer who had cut the line went on about how important it was for people to respect food allergies, Beth heard someone in the gaggle of girls mention Jack's name. For a moment, she froze, not sure what to do. The right thing was to move out of earshot because eavesdropping was wrong. Instead, she took a step closer, her back to them as she made an event of getting some paper napkins from a holder on the counter and listened closely.

"How was it?" one of the girls behind Beth asked.

"He seems like he's so much fun. Is he fun?" another asked.

"I bet he tried to kiss you. My sister said Jack Lehman has kissed more girls in Kent County than any other boy."

"But not you, Dorcas," someone added. They all giggled in unison.

"Come on, Barbara. Tell us how your date

with Jack was. As soon as I get my pretzel, I need to meet my brother at the buggy."

Clutching the handful of napkins, Beth looked over her shoulder. The moment she saw the petite girl this time, she realized who she was.

It was Barbara Troyer.

The same Barbara Troyer who had come between Jack and Willa.

Chapter Fourteen

Shaking, Beth walked away. Behind her, she heard Lettie at the pretzel stand call her name, but she kept going. Jane spotted her and joined her in the aisle packed with shoppers.

"Let's go," Beth said, trying not to cry. She didn't want to fall apart in a public place where so many people knew her and her family.

Jane carried a big box of fresh donuts. "What's wrong?"

Beth shook her head, unable to answer. If she could only make it home, she'd be *oll recht*. She would survive this. She could survive Jack cheating on her and their breakup. It had been inevitable from the beginning; she realized that now. She didn't know why she had thought it would work.

You can't make a silk purse out of a sow's ear. That's what her *mam* used to say.

Willa had warned Beth that Jack was a two-timer, and Rosie told her that he was a player. He'd probably taken advantage of that widow, too.

Beth hurried down the noisy, crowded aisle. "Where's Willa?" she murmured.

Jane grabbed Beth's arm, looked at her face, and her lighthearted demeanor changed. "I'll find her," she said, not asking her what was wrong again. "You go to the buggy."

But as the deli came into view, they saw Willa. She was talking to an Amish boy her age and he was smiling at her as she was at him.

Jane darted from the crowd of customers that moved them as if they were in a flowing river. "Willa! Let's go." Balancing the donuts in one hand, Jane grabbed her sister's arm and led her away. "Sorry," Jane told the boy with a quick smile. "She has to go home!"

Willa tried to resist, but even though Jane was small, she was strong and Willa couldn't escape her grasp. "What are you doing?" Willa demanded peevishly. "I have another fifteen minutes. We aren't supposed to meet for fifteen minutes!"

"Beth has to go." Jane pushed the windowed box of donuts at Willa and slipped her arm through Beth's. "Almost there, Beth," she murmured in a calm, protective voice.

Willa hurried to catch up. "What is going on?" she demanded, looking over her shoulder at the confused young man Jane had taken her from. "This isn't fair. Beth, you said half an hour and—" She met Beth's gaze and went quiet.

Her eyes filling with tears, Beth shifted her focus to the floor in front of her. *One foot in front of the other,* she told herself.

"What is going on?" Willa repeated. Then looking from one sister to the other, she said, "Out with it. Both of you." She grabbed Jane's free arm and steered her sisters into an alcove where there was an ATM machine. She shoved the box of donuts back at Jane and blocked Beth's escape. "Tell me what happened, Beth, because something happened, otherwise you would be in this state. I've never seen you like this."

Beth had it in her head not to tell her family what happened until she was home safely. At home, she could fall apart and those who loved her most in the world would be there for her. But the words tumbled out of her. In a few sentences, she managed to tell her sisters what she had just seen and heard.

"Oh, Beth," Jane cried, rubbing Beth's arm soothingly. "It will be *oll recht*. Let's get you to the buggy and—"

"Where is she?" Willa interrupted angrily. This was a side of Willa that Beth couldn't remember ever seeing.

Beth stared at her sister, who was only a year older than she was. "What?" she asked, confused by the question.

"Where is she?" Willa demanded through clenched teeth. "Barbara Troyer."

Beth didn't know why her sister wanted to know where the exchange had occurred, but she wasn't thinking clearly. The market was loud and there were so many people that she felt claustrophobic. "Um…pretzel stand," Beth managed.

Willa whirled around to Jane. "Take her to the buggy. I'll meet you there." Then, as she turned to go, she leaned closer, making eye contact with Beth, and said gently, "Go to the buggy with Jane. I'll be there in a minute." She strode away. "This isn't going to take long."

Jane walked Beth to their family's buggy, one arm around her and the other clutching her box of pink frosted donuts with pink and white sprinkles. As Jane got them settled in the back, Beth stared out the window, anger beginning to bubble up inside her. The moment they reached home, she would march down to the store and fire Jack. Right on the spot. And she wasn't going to allow him to sweet-talk her with any *perfectly logical* explanations this time.

Jack was all the things Rosie, Willa and everyone else in Kent County had said about him, and Beth had been a fool to believe a word he said. She'd fire him so she never had to speak to him again. She'd hire someone else to finish the store. She'd have Eleanor pay what they owed him, minus the finished work that wasn't complete and that would be the end of it. Decision made, Beth's anger subsided, and she began to feel numb again. Which feeling was worse, she didn't know.

By the time Willa climbed up into the driver's seat, Beth was staring out the window, her eyes focused on nothing. Her heart hadn't simply broken. It had shattered.

"I knew it," Willa said, shutting the door.

"She's not feeling well," Jane said from one of the two backseats that ran perpendicular to the front bench seat. "She said she feels sick to her stomach. That she might be sick."

"You shouldn't get sick. You should get mad." Willa grabbed both of Beth's hands and Beth stared at her sister, feeling as if she were floating and couldn't find purchase.

"She lied," Willa declared. "I knew it! A girl like her, she'll do anything to get a man like Jack."

Beth blinked. "I don't understand."

"Barbara Troyer," Willa said in disgust. She still held tightly to Beth's hands. "What you heard a few minutes ago? It was all a lie. A lie fat enough and mean enough that Barbara better make an appointment to see her bishop."

Beth hadn't been able to look at Willa or even really focus, but now she met her gaze. She'd never seen Willa like this, so angry, so... driven.

"Barbara just admitted it to me. She made up the whole story about being out with Jack over the weekend."

Jane thrust her head over the seat. She smelled of donut frosting. "Wait. Barbara told you she lied? How did you get her to admit that in front of her friends?"

"I didn't." Willa turned to Jane. "I told her we could talk privately or in front of her friends. Her choice." She touched the corner of her mouth. "You've got pink icing here."

She looked back at Beth. "It was interesting how quick Barbara excused herself from her friends. She seemed startled. I guess she's never had anyone confront her about her lies before."

"She lied?" Beth repeated the word, feeling the blood return to her face. A moment ago, she'd been cold and unable to concentrate on any single thought for more than a second.

"*Ya*, she lied," Willa said indignantly. "She started the rumor about her dating Jack at Masts' barn raising. I heard something about it yesterday from Millie's friend Annie but we all agreed it was more idle gossip. I've learned a lot about Barbara since Jack and I broke up, and little of it is good. Anyway, I guess the rumors about her dating Jack again weren't traveling fast enough to suit her, so she's telling groups of people at a time."

Beth frowned, trying to wrap her head around what her sister was saying. "So she didn't go out with Jack over the weekend when he said he couldn't see me because he had to work for his *dat*?"

"*Nay*, she didn't go out with Jack," Willa scoffed. "Not in months, at least. Not since he started building the store. What would make you think Jack would go out with her? He's madly in love with you, Beth. He's all puppy-eyes anytime he's near you."

"I've seen it, too," Jane agreed, wiping her mouth with a paper napkin. "Mad in love with you. Cora says he's going to ask you to marry him any day. *Dat* keeps saying he has a secret about you, and then he giggles. We're sure Jack must have asked *Dat* for your hand."

Beth looked at Jane and then back at Willa, still trying to unravel so much information at once. "And Barbara confessed all of this to you?" she asked Willa suspiciously.

Willa smirked. "I think I scared her. I think she was afraid I would slap her in front of her friends."

"Willa!" Jane reprimanded from the back of the buggy. "There's never, ever a reason to resort to violence. *Mam* and *Dat* taught us that from the time we were babies."

Willa glanced at Jane. "I didn't say I *was* going to slap her. Though she would deserve it."

Beth stared through the windshield at their driving horse patiently waiting to be untied from the hitching post. "So Jack didn't do anything wrong?" she asked.

Willa shook her head. "He didn't."

Tears filled Beth's eyes. "*Ach*, I've made a

terrible mistake. How could I have mistrusted him?" She looked at her older sister. "He is a *goot* man, isn't he?"

Willa squeezed Beth's hand. "He is." She hesitated and then went on. "You know, I'm still sad it didn't work out between us. I liked him, but I know now that he wasn't meant for me because *Gott* meant him for you. And I wish all the happiness in the world for the two of you."

"Aww, that's sweet, Willa," Jane said.

Beth pressed both hands to her cheeks. "I was going to break up with him as soon as we got home." She shook her head, thinking of how close she had come to destroying her relationship with Jack. Ruining both of their lives and all because she'd overheard something. "I was going to fire him."

"You were really going to fire him? Without telling Ellie?" Jane took a bite from another donut. "Anyone want one?" She held up the box.

Willa pushed it back. "I thought you bought them for your sewing circle tomorrow."

"I did. But they're so *goot*. I'll make pecan sticky buns instead."

Willa returned her attention to Beth. "So everything is all right. You don't have to say a word to him about Barbara. You didn't break up with him or fire him. He never has to know how close he came to losing his job and his girlfriend."

"*Nay*," Beth said, folding her hands in her lap. "I have to tell him, because this isn't the first time I believed what other people told me about him. Even though I know they couldn't be true because I know him, I let other people's words sway my heart." Her voice caught in her throat. "I can't believe I've been suspicious of him when he was innocent all along. What a terrible person I am."

"You are *not* a terrible person," Willa said, shaking her head.

"Then why would I think such things?"

Willa shrugged. "Maybe because you're scared. I've never been in love, but I would guess it's scary. How can it not be? You want to be sure you're making the right choice when you marry before *Gott*."

Beth was crying again, but now her tears were of happiness. "How did you get to be so smart, *schweschter*?" she asked Willa.

Willa laughed. "I think that's the first time anyone has ever called me that." She peered into Beth's face. "Ready to go home?"

"*Ya*. But I want you to let me off at the end

of the lane. I need to apologize to Jack and… and tell him I love him."

Jane clapped loudly from behind Beth. "Oh, goodie, can I go with you?"

"*Nay*," Willa and Beth told their sister in unison.

And they all dissolved into laughter.

Chapter Fifteen

By the time the Koffman sisters reached home, Beth had wiped away her tears and was eager to talk to Jack. Her heart was so light that she was giddy with excitement to see him. On the way, as Willa and Jane discussed their favorite donuts, Beth planned what she would say to Jack.

The first thing Beth wanted to do was apologize to Jack for doubting his character. She shouldn't have judged him by what others said. It didn't matter that her sister and her best friend had planted the seeds of doubt about his character. Beth should have trusted her instincts, mainly because Jack had been so open and honest whenever she questioned him about his past.

Willa had barely pulled the buggy to a stop at the end of their lane when Beth leaped down.

Jane climbed up front and stuck her head out the window. "Are you sure I can't go with you?" she called.

Beth smiled at Jane, proud of how she had handled her meltdown. When had her little sister become so mature and capable? Somehow Jane had known something was wrong with Beth, but instead of grilling her, she'd leapt into action. "You may not join my beau and me in a private conversation that will likely end in discussing marriage."

"Ohh!" Jane's eyes grew round with excitement as she hung out the open door. "Do you think Jack will ask you to marry him?"

"I don't know." Beth met Willa's eyes, a twinkle in her own. "I might ask *him*."

Jane was so shocked that she fell back against the seat and Willa urged their driving horse forward.

Beth raised her hand in a goodbye, feeling so blessed to have such wonderful sisters. "See you later!"

"Come home as soon as you can," Jane hollered as the buggy rolled away. "I want to hear *everything*!"

As Beth walked across the neatly mowed grass toward the store, her heartbeat quickened. It wasn't as much from nervousness as excitement. She would tell Jack how sorry she was for her false judgments and promise never to question his integrity again. Then she was going to confess she loved him. Why must the man always be the one to declare his love first? Why did a man always have to take on such an emotional burden, wondering if they would be rejected? If their marriage was to be one of equals, as she wanted, shouldn't that begin before vows are exchanged?

Beth had been teasing Jane when she said she would ask Jack to marry her, but she might bring up the subject, depending on how the conversation went. If he said he was in love with her as well, she saw no reason to wait.

Beth knew that Jack was worried about finances and suspected he would want to delay the wedding until he was more stable financially. But plenty of couples married without a hundred dollars between them. *Gott* meant for man and woman to marry. If they married before Him, he would provide food and shelter. She and Jack could figure out the logistics later. She knew she would be unable to live under his father's roof because of the older man's temperament. Her *dat* or Eleanor would never agree to the marriage under those circumstances, but she and Jack had options.

Maybe they could live with her family for a while, or better yet, above the store. The plan had been to eventually build a small apartment for rental income in the open space on the second floor.

As Beth approached the store, she saw Jack, Lemuel, Mark and the new hire sitting under the shade of the front porch. They were eating their midday meal from black metal lunch pails. There was no sign of her father.

"*Guder mariye*," she called as she crossed the grass, taking care not to walk on the newly laid brick sidewalk.

Sitting in a wrought iron chair at a table Millie had found at a yard sale, Jack grinned at her and took a bite of his sandwich. "It's afternoon for those of us who have been on the job since six this morning." There was a tone of irritation in his voice that surprised her.

"*Guder nummadaag*, then." She smiled at him. He was wearing his usual work clothes: heavy boots, a straw hat and dark sunglasses. But to her, he was the most handsome, charming man she had ever known. And she loved him, and she wasn't afraid to admit it to herself or anyone else. Now that she had leaped that hurdle, she realized that fear of her feelings for him had played a part in looking for the worst in Jack. She was afraid to love him, and, on some level, she was trying in her head to make him unlovable.

"*Dat* gone home already?" Beth asked Jack.

"*Ya*, he lost his lunch. Millie said he had it when they left the house so we have no idea what he did with it. She took him home to eat." He didn't make eye contact with her as he spoke. "I offered to let him share my lunch. My *mam* always packs enough for three men, but Felty looked tired and Millie thought he'd been out in the sun too long. I suspect she used his missing lunch as an excuse to get him home."

Beth studied Jack's handsome face, trying to figure out what was wrong. She hadn't talked to him since the previous morning when they'd had spent half an hour together going over the types of trim that would go around the doors and window frames. Everything seemed to be okay between them then. He'd invited her to run errands in Dover with him on Saturday and then they were going to get pizza.

"Can we talk?" Beth asked Jack hesitantly. Her newfound confidence had waned.

"I think that would be a good idea." He rose without looking at her. "Let's go inside. Cooler."

As Beth crossed the porch to follow him

through the open front door, she noticed that the other men kept their gazes fixed elsewhere. No one said a word.

It *was* cooler in the store's main room, which ran the entire width of the building because the large windows provided cross-ventilation. The walls were a bright white called Snowbound that she had chosen herself and it still smelled of fresh paint.

Beth suddenly felt nervous and unsure of herself and wondered if this was the wrong time to have the discussion she had planned. Jack was preoccupied and didn't seem to be in the mood for a heart-to-heart conversation. Maybe she should postpone it until Saturday, when they would have the whole afternoon together. It wasn't fair to ask him to switch gears and discuss personal matters when he was at work.

She ran her hand along the long counter where customers would check out their purchases. Stalling, she ran her hand along the smooth walnut top. "This came out beautifully. It's even prettier than I expected. I like the beadboard on the front," she observed.

He stood a few feet behind her, saying nothing.

Beth turned to him, digging deeply for all

the courage she could muster. "Jack, something happened today that made me realize—" When she looked at him and saw an unreceptive look on his face, she gulped. "I was at Spence's this morning and ran into Barbara Troyer and—"

"Funny you should bring up Barbara Troyer," Jack interrupted. "Because I wanted to talk to you about her, too." He slid his hands into his front pockets. "Not exactly about her, but…" He stared at the newly laid walnut floorboards that had yet to be stained. "I think we're done here."

Beth furrowed her brow, confused. She glanced around. "You're almost done, but you said it would be another week before the trim was up and painted, and you put polyurethane on the floors. Plus that back door—"

"I'm not talking about finishing the store. I'm talking about us, Beth." He pulled his hand out of his pocket to pass it through the air. "You and me, we're done."

This time he did not look away from her but instead met her gaze head-on. She saw sparks of anger in his blue eyes that made her heart tumble.

"Jack," she murmured.

But he kept talking. "In line at the feedstore

after work yesterday, I heard that Barbara and I are dating again. Also that I kicked a widow out of her house so I could demolish it and build a duplex. Apparently, I already have a contract on it and stand to make a pretty penny."

"Jack, I don't believe any of those things."

"Of course you don't, because you and your sisters have been making up these lies and passing them around."

Beth drew back. "What?" She shook her head, hurt that he would accuse her of such a thing. "*Nay*, I have not said anything like that to anyone. I would never do that, Jack." She pressed her hand to her chest. "I would never do that to you." She bit down on her lower lip. "And my sister would never make up lies about you or anyone else. *Ya*, they might like to gossip," she conceded, "but they would never start a rumor."

He hesitated. "*Oll recht*, but you've heard this gossip. Heard ridiculous lies that folks have been passing around for months, years, lies your sisters shared. And you didn't defend me, Beth." His voice caught in his throat and he took a breath before going on. "Not only did you listen to these lies, but you didn't speak up for me. You didn't tell people like your friend Rosie that she shouldn't be talking about things she doesn't know about. About people she doesn't know. You *know* me better than anyone else, yet you didn't defend me." He hadn't raised his voice, and when he spoke again, it was even softer. "I would never do that to you, Beth." He set his jaw. "I thought we would marry. I thought we would be good together, make a good team." He shook his head. "But how can I enter into a union that will last a lifetime and beyond with a woman who doesn't have my back?"

Beth hung her head, tears stinging her eyes. Everything he said was true, at least to a degree. She hadn't gossiped about him, not even before they began dating. But she had undoubtedly heard things about him, believed them enough to ask him about them. Accuse him.

She felt ashamed. How did she get to this place? Why had she not told Rosie it was wrong to talk about him? After she heard Jack's side of the story, why hadn't she confronted Willa? Why hadn't she told her sister that it was wrong to present her side of their breakup in a way that made him look bad?

"I'm sorry," she whispered. "I didn't mean—"

"You know what," Jack said, talking over her. Now he had raised his voice. "I'm done here. I quit."

She had been staring at the floor, but her head snapped as she heard what he said. He was quitting? "You can't quit. The store is almost done."

"I can quit. I won't work for a family like the Koffmans. Not for the Koffman girls, at least. Your *dat* has nothing to do with this and I'll tell him so."

"Jack." She took a step toward him and reached out to grasp his arms. "Please. I'm sorry. I'm so sorry. You're right. I've made so many mistakes over the last months, but—"

Jack backed away. "It's too late for *sorrys*." He strode toward the front door. "We'll finish out the day. That's it. I'll bring Eleanor a final bill in a couple of days." He walked out onto the front porch and slammed the door behind him.

Beth stood there for a long moment, her devastation so profound that she knew this had to be a nightmare. She'd soon wake and still have a lifetime with Jack ahead of her.

But then she heard the rumble of Jack's voice as he spoke to the men outside and she knew this was worse than any nightmare she could have imagined. Tears streaming down her face, she ran out the back door and headed for home.

Chapter Sixteen

Beth sat on the window seat in her father's bedroom and listened to the pitter-pat of rain on the glass. It had been raining for days, unusual for late July, and it looked as dreary outside as she felt on the inside. She sighed and leaned her cheek against the wall.

She'd come upstairs to change her *dat*'s bedsheets, but now that it was done, she couldn't bring herself to join the fray downstairs. Her sisters who were home were in the middle of canning corn, and Cora and Eleanor were arguing when she came upstairs. And again, it was about Cora applying for the teaching position that would open for the fall. All her sisters could be stubborn, but those two were particularly tenacious, and so far, neither had given in.

Beth closed her eyes, wishing she could

crawl into bed although it wasn't even lunchtime yet. Not to sleep but to hide under her quilt from the world. From herself and her devastation. It had been six days since Jack broke up with her and she had not heard from him. She had cried every day. The hardest part was that she couldn't blame him for what he'd done. All blame for the breakup fell squarely on her shoulders. She and Jack had been given the opportunity to build a wonderful life together and she had ruined it. She had been foolish in her words and thoughts and her penance was to lose the only man she would ever love.

Since the breakup, Beth had obsessed over every word she and Jack had exchanged over the last few months, the good conversations and the bad. She remembered every kind, sweet or funny thing he had said to her. And every terrible accusation she had made. She had prayed for hours each day for *Gott*'s forgiveness and Jack's. She had also foolishly prayed that all would somehow turn out right even after everything she had done to undermine their relationship. She couldn't see how that could happen, but didn't the Bible say that all things were possible with *Gott*?

So she kept praying. She knew that Jack would never love her now, but if he could forgive her, perhaps she could find her way forward, at least content that there were no ill feelings between them. That remote possibility made her clasp her hands, close her eyes and pray.

Beth didn't know how much time had passed when she whispered Amen and opened her eyes. She rose, realizing that if she didn't get downstairs with the dirty sheets, a sister would come looking for her and she didn't want to worry them. She appreciated her family's concern. She didn't know how she could have gotten through the last week without their kind words, hugs and mutual commiseration.

Beth leaned forward to look out the window one last time before she joined her family and, to her surprise, saw an Amish man in a black raincoat walking up their lane. His head was down so that his broad-brimmed hat shielded his face from the falling rain. She wondered who would be on foot on a day like this.

Then she realized who it was.

Beth would have known that walk anywhere. It was Jack. Her Jack.

Nay, he was no longer *her* Jack she thought, and tears welled in her eyes.

She leaned closer to the window and her breath frosted the cool glass. Pressing her hand to her chest, where she could feel her heart beating fast, she wondered what to do. Though she wanted to believe he'd come to see her and make amends, she knew better. She'd been expecting his visit all week but not because she was silly enough to believe he would come to tell her he had forgiven her and wanted to marry her. He'd come with his final bill so that Eleanor could pay him.

The wise thing would be to remain where she was until she saw Jack walking away from the house. She could make herself busy dusting and tidying her *dat's* room until he left, sparing them any awkwardness.

Her gaze shifted to the driveway below. Watching Jack, her heart aching for what she had lost, she balled her hands into fists and tried to find the strength to stay put.

Head down against the pouring rain, Jack strode up the driveway, thankful for the raincoat his *mam* had insisted he take. Mark had dropped him off at the Koffmans' and would be back in half an hour to pick him up. Then they were headed to an Amish sawmill in Hickory Grove to place a large lumber order. With prep work to be done before he began a new addition for an Englisher he'd just signed the contract on, he was thankful for another day of rain. It gave him time to make calculations and prepare plans for the architect.

The dreary day also seemed appropriate for the way he felt. He's been miserable for a week now. Even though he felt justified in breaking up with Beth, his heart was broken. He loved her. If he hadn't been sure of that before, he knew it now. He missed her so much that his chest ached. He was so miserable that he was again contemplating joining his grandfather in Wisconsin. As if putting hundreds of miles between him and Beth would make the breakup any easier.

He'd set the plans on hold, for now, knowing he wasn't in the right frame of mind to make such a monumental decision. Instead, he concentrated on his business right here in Kent County. In the last week, he'd not only secured the contract for the addition but met with three potential new clients, who all seemed eager to sign contracts when they saw how reasonable his estimates were.

Almost at the Koffman house, Jack couldn't decide if he wanted Beth to answer the door or not. On the one hand, he desperately wanted to see her. On the other, it would only cause more pain, wouldn't it?

Sensing someone was watching him, he glanced at the first-story windows. Nothing. But then he saw movement in an upstairs window. It was only the flash of a green dress; it could have been any of the seven Koffman sisters. But what if it was Beth? Would she come down to greet him or stay upstairs?

He wouldn't blame her if she remained hidden from him while he conducted his business with Felty and Eleanor. But what if she wanted to see him? What if she wanted to talk?

As Jack reached the back porch, he almost turned around and went back down the lane. Suddenly he couldn't remember what had set him off the previous week. What could Beth have said or done that was so terrible they couldn't find their way through it together with *Gott*'s help? Why had he allowed temporary emotions to make such a permanent decision?

His hand trembled as he knocked on the door. Behind it, he heard female voices, then footsteps. The door opened and it was Jane. When she saw him, her face lit up.

"Jack! *Ach*, thank the heavens you're here. I've tried to get Beth to talk to you, but I think she's too scared. Now you can be brave for both of you, can't you?"

Jack stood there frozen as Jane chattered,

not sure what to say. Knowing Beth was somewhere in the house, a hundred thoughts flew through his head and he couldn't grasp a single one. He lowered his gaze and cleared his throat. "I'm here to speak to your *dat* and Eleanor."

"Nonsense." She crossed her arms. "You and I both know who you're here to see."

"Um, I brought the bill. For the balance on the store." He fumbled in his pocket for the carefully handwritten sheet of paper.

"If you say so," she quipped, obviously not believing him.

And now that he was here, he wasn't sure he believed it either. The night before, he'd had a heart-to-heart talk with his mother about the breakup with Beth. When he told her how lost he felt, she'd insisted the cure was prayer. She'd reminded him that the response should be prayer whenever a man or woman felt lost in the Paran Desert. And so he had prayed a simple prayer. He had asked *Gott* to make him whole again.

Jane opened the door farther. "So come on with you." She waved him in. "And give me that wet coat. You drip water on Ellie's clean floor and we're both in trouble."

She stepped back to allow him entry, and he

dutifully handed over his raincoat, thinking how different the Koffman girls were from his sisters. There were no shy, meek women here.

"Look who's finally arrived," Jane announced, leading Jack from their mudroom to the kitchen. "Shall I fetch Beth?" She halted suddenly, glancing in the direction of the hall that led to the remainder of the house. "Ah, there she is, so no need."

When Jack saw Beth, his legs grew weak, and he struggled to fight the emotion that rose from his chest, threatening to strangle him in his throat. *His Beth*. He had missed her so much. When he set out, his only intention was to collect the money owed to him. Now all he wanted to do was beg Beth for her forgiveness. It was true that she had hurt him by participating in the gossip about him, if only because she hadn't stood up for him. And she *had* questioned his integrity when he felt she knew him too well for that. But she had apologized. And his response had been in petty anger. He had taken a small hurt and turned it into a broken heart. Two broken hearts, he suspected by the look on her face.

Now what did he do? His gaze met Beth's. She looked tired, but the shadows under her eyes made her no less beautiful.

"Jack," Eleanor said as she turned from the stove, wiping her hands on her apron.

Millie, Cora, Jane and Willa were all looking at him. Only Henry and Felty were absent.

The kitchen smelled of sweet corn and every surface of the room was covered with the trappings of canning the vegetable. There were glass jars everywhere, some filled with bi-color corn, others empty. There were baskets of husks and ears of corn yet to be husked on the floor and chairs. On the huge stove, pots bubbled with water for sterilization and blanching corn.

"Girls, can you give us a minute?" Eleanor asked, glancing around at her sisters.

"Can't we stay?" Jane whined, at last showing her age.

"Come on. Let's give them some privacy." Millie linked her arm through Jane's. "Willa, Cora and I will play a game of Dutch Blitz with you."

"But I'd rather stay here," Jane protested.

All four sisters left the kitchen, passing by Beth, who stood in the kitchen entryway as still as a garden statue. When Jack shifted his gaze, hoping to make eye contact, she looked down at the floor. But she made no attempt to leave the room.

That was a good thing, wasn't it?

Jack swallowed and looked at Eleanor. When he spoke, he kept his tone businesslike and without emotion. "I, um…brought the bill." He held it up.

"Excellent." She smiled at him as if nothing was unusual about the request for payment before he'd completed the job. "Let me get our checkbook." She walked out of the kitchen, passing Beth. "Be right back. Beth, could you pull that last batch out of the water and rinse it so it doesn't overcook?"

Then Jack and Beth were alone.

When Eleanor walked out of the kitchen, leaving Beth alone with Jack, Beth considered running upstairs. She had prayed Jack would come all week, and now that he was here, she didn't know what to say. What to do.

But if she left the corn on the stove, it would be ruined. It was a waste of time to can overcooked corn; it would turn to mush in the final processing stage. So she made herself walk to the stove. With her back to Jack, she said, "Hello," as she grabbed hot mitts from the counter and lifted the colander from the pot to drain the corn.

"Hello," he answered, his tone so cool that

she closed her eyes, steadying herself for fear of dropping the colander.

He was angry with her, and why shouldn't he be? She wouldn't blame him if he never spoke to her again.

She walked to the large farmhouse sink, set the colander down and turned on the cold water to rinse off the corn kernels and stop the cooking process. Behind her, Jack said nothing. He stood there, and the silence of the kitchen stretched between them until it was as taut as a rubber band pulled too tightly.

Beth now regretted coming downstairs. Seeing Jack only made her feel worse. And he certainly didn't look happy. She should have spared both their feelings.

Footsteps sounded in the hallways and Beth exhaled with relief. Eleanor had found the checkbook at last and—*nay*, she realized. It wasn't Eleanor. It was their *dat*.

"Jack!" her *vadde*r greeted enthusiastically. "Where have you been? Store's almost done, but we've still got work to do. The doorframes all need a second coat of paint."

Beth turned around to see her father giving Jack a hearty hug. "*Dat*," she said, embarrassed. Since the breakup, he hadn't asked her about Jack, so she hadn't mentioned it. Eventually, when he did ask, she'd keep it simple and tell him they'd parted ways and let the subject drop.

"Good to see you, Felty."

Beth was surprised to see Jack hug her father in return. It was something she wasn't sure she had ever witnessed between Amish men.

"Been wondering where you got to." Her father stepped back. "What can I do for you?"

Jack looked at Beth's father, then at her.

"*Dat*," she repeated. "Jack has come for his final payment. For the store."

Her father frowned. "But he's not done yet!" He looked to Jack. "You're not done yet, *sohn*."

Beth set aside the hot mitts and went to her father. "Jack's not going to do any more work on the store. We're going to hire someone else to finish up."

Her father's brow furrowed into deep grooves. "Why would he do that?" Again he turned to Jack. "What would make you do that?"

Beth closed her eyes and wished she was anywhere but there. She took a breath and opened them. "*Dat*," she said gently, the words paining her. "Jack and I aren't...we aren't together anymore. It would be too awkward for both of us."

"Not together anymore?" He almost shouted

the words. "That's ridiculous. You love him," he told Beth. Then to Jack he said, "And you love her."

To Beth's surprise, Jack hung his head. But then he lifted it and said, "You're right, Felty, I do love Beth." He looked at her.

And that was Beth's undoing. Tears ran down her cheeks. "I love you, too," she murmured, holding his gaze.

Jack walked over to her. "Beth, I know that you never really believed the things people said about me."

"I didn't," she cried. "Last week, when I went to see you, it was to apologize for ever considering you could be anyone other than the man I know." She looked down, feeling a blush of shame creep across her cheeks. "I don't know why I was so quick to consider every word of gossip about you when I knew who you were and knew you couldn't have done those things. I think I was afraid. Afraid of loving you." She whispered the last words.

"*Ach*, Beth." Jack took her hands in his and gazed into her eyes. "Maybe that's why I walked away last week instead of trying to have a genuine conversation. I think I was afraid, too."

"Of what?" she asked.

"The same as you. Of loving someone. Of making the commitment before *Gott* to be your husband. I think I was afraid I wasn't good enough for you." He looked down. "Someone tells you for long enough that you're not good enough, that you'll never be good enough, you begin to believe it."

Beth knew he was referring to his father. It was a matter they'd discussed several times. "I'm so sorry," she said sincerely. She was sorry for all of it. For what she had done and for how his father treated him.

Her father clapped his hands together so loudly that it startled her and Jack.

"So what's the problem then?" he demanded. Then to Jack he said, "You want that land?"

"Um, *ya*, I think I do." Still holding her hands, he looked into Beth's eyes. "If your daughter will be my wife, I think we'll need it."

Beth's heart was pounding with joy. "What land? What are you talking about?" she asked.

"A few weeks ago your *dat* offered to give us a couple of acres of land near the store. So I can build us a house."

Fresh tears ran down Beth's cheeks. "A house?"

Jack pulled her into his arms right in front of her father. "Say you'll marry me, Beth. Marry me, and I vow to be a good husband and make you the happiest woman in Honeycomb. In the county."

She laughed through her tears and hugged him tightly. "*Ya*, I'll marry you."

"*Goot.*" Her *dat* clapped Jack on the back as he walked by them. "And now that that's settled, let's have some tea and cookies." He shuffled toward the pantry. "I know where Ellie hides the cookies." He tapped a finger to his temple. "She thinks she's clever but where does she think she got that?"

Beth gazed into Jack's eyes and realized *Gott* had answered her prayers.

He always did.

Epilogue

Four months later

At the end of the lane, Beth waved to Millie and her new husband, Elden, as they crossed the road, a swinging lantern to light their way. Then she slipped her arm through Jack's. Gazing up at him, she still couldn't believe that she was now Beth Lehman, a married woman. In some ways, it seemed as if it had all happened so quickly, yet at other times, it had felt as if the day would never come.

It was Elden and Millie who had proposed a double wedding. At first, Beth had refused. She didn't want to take a single moment of joy from her older sister, who had been engaged a year. But Millie had insisted that for them to share a wedding day would only increase her happiness. Besides, she'd pointed out with a smile that there would be less work for Eleanor to throw one wedding in her home rather than two.

"Ready to go home, wife?" Jack asked, his smile as handsome as ever.

"I am, husband."

"Good thing we don't have to go far," he said as they began to walk toward the store.

After they agreed to wed, Jack had worked every weekend and night building them an apartment over the now-operational Koffman's General Store. The plan was to build a house on their land on the edge of her father's property in a year or two, but the one-bedroom apartment was perfect for them to begin their new life together.

"Going to get cold tonight," Jack went on. "We might even see some snow flurries."

She gazed into his gorgeous green eyes. "Good thing Henry started a fire in our new woodstove," Even though they'd been planning this day for months, she still couldn't believe that Jack was at last her husband.

"Good thing," he agreed. "Because I can't wait to kiss my wife for the first time."

Beth halted and turned to him. An automatic lamp on the side of the building came on and they stood in a circle of light. "What?"

she teased. "You've never kissed your wife before?"

He shook his head. "I haven't, but in all fairness, she's only been my wife for ten hours."

"Hmm," Beth said. "Well, do you want to kiss her?"

A half smile crept across his face. He was so handsome in his Sunday black suit, heavy black coat and wide-brimmed wool hat. "*Ya*, I want to kiss her. I've wanted to kiss her since the day she told me off in public at a feedstore."

Beth grinned back and then feigned gravity. "But do you think she wants to kiss you?"

The look on his face told her he wasn't entirely sure if she was being serious or not. "I think she does. I hope she does."

Feeling shy, she whispered. "I know she does."

And then her husband kissed her, and with that single, long-awaited kiss, Beth knew that her life would be filled with laughter, love and kisses.

* * * * *

Dear Reader,

Thank you for joining the Koffman sisters and me in Honeycomb again!

My goodness, Beth and Jack had their troubles, didn't they? But I loved how they were eventually able to forgive their own failings and each other's. And they are so well matched. If any young, married couple can navigate the modern world the Old Order Amish are facing, it's Beth and Jack.

As to what will happen next in the Koffman household, you'll have to come back and visit. A little bird told me that Cora is not going to give up the idea of teaching school easily. But what will she do when the mysterious Tobit Lapp arrives in Honeycomb, expecting to be hired for the same job?

I hope to see you again soon.

Blessings,
Emma Miller

Get 4 FREE REWARDS!

We'll send you 2 FREE Books plus 2 FREE Mystery Gifts.

FREE
Value Over
$20

Both the **Love Inspired®** and **Love Inspired® Suspense** series feature compelling novels filled with inspirational romance, faith, forgiveness and hope.

YES! Please send me 2 FREE novels from the Love Inspired or Love Inspired Suspense series and my 2 FREE gifts (gifts are worth about $10 retail). After receiving them, if I don't wish to receive any more books, I can return the shipping statement marked "cancel." If I don't cancel, I will receive 6 brand-new Love Inspired Larger-Print books or Love Inspired Suspense Larger-Print books every month and be billed just $6.49 each in the U.S. or $6.74 each in Canada. That is a savings of at least 16% off the cover price. It's quite a bargain! Shipping and handling is just 50¢ per book in the U.S. and $1.25 per book in Canada.* I understand that accepting the 2 free books and gifts places me under no obligation to buy anything. I can always return a shipment and cancel at any time by calling the number below. The free books and gifts are mine to keep no matter what I decide.

Choose one: ☐ **Love Inspired**
Larger-Print
(122/322 IDN GRHK)

☐ **Love Inspired Suspense**
Larger-Print
(107/307 IDN GRHK)

Name (please print)

Address   Apt. #

City   State/Province   Zip/Postal Code

Email: Please check this box ☐ if you would like to receive newsletters and promotional emails from Harlequin Enterprises ULC and its affiliates. You can unsubscribe anytime.

Mail to the **Harlequin Reader Service:**
IN U.S.A.: P.O. Box 1341, Buffalo, NY 14240-8531
IN CANADA: P.O. Box 603, Fort Erie, Ontario L2A 5X3

Want to try 2 free books from another series! Call 1-800-873-8635 or visit www.ReaderService.com.

*Terms and prices subject to change without notice. Prices do not include sales taxes, which will be charged (if applicable) based on your state or country of residence. Canadian residents will be charged applicable taxes. Offer not valid in Quebec. This offer is limited to one order per household. Books received may not be as shown. Not valid for current subscribers to the Love Inspired or Love Inspired Suspense series. All orders subject to approval. Credit or debit balances in a customer's account(s) may be offset by any other outstanding balance owed by or to the customer. Please allow 4 to 6 weeks for delivery. Offer available while quantities last.

Your Privacy—Your information is being collected by Harlequin Enterprises ULC, operating as Harlequin Reader Service. For a complete summary of the information we collect, how we use this information and to whom it is disclosed, please visit our privacy notice located at corporate.harlequin.com/privacy-notice. From time to time we may also exchange your personal information with reputable third parties. If you wish to opt out of this sharing of your personal information, please visit readerservice.com/consumerschoice or call 1-800-873-8635. **Notice to California Residents**—Under California law, you have specific rights to control and access your data. For more information on these rights and how to exercise them, visit corporate.harlequin.com/california-privacy.

LIRLIS22R3

Get 4 FREE REWARDS!

We'll send you 2 FREE Books plus 2 FREE Mystery Gifts.

FREE Value Over **$20**

Both the **Harlequin® Special Edition** and **Harlequin® Heartwarming™** series feature compelling novels filled with stories of love and strength where the bonds of friendship, family and community unite.

YES! Please send me 2 FREE novels from the Harlequin Special Edition or Harlequin Heartwarming series and my 2 FREE gifts (gifts are worth about $10 retail). After receiving them, if I don't wish to receive any more books, I can return the shipping statement marked "cancel." If I don't cancel, I will receive 6 brand-new Harlequin Special Edition books every month and be billed just $5.49 each in the U.S. or $6.24 each in Canada, a savings of at least 12% off the cover price, or 4 brand-new Harlequin Heartwarming Larger-Print books every month and be billed just $6.24 each in the U.S. or $6.74 each in Canada, a savings of at least 19% off the cover price. It's quite a bargain! Shipping and handling is just 50¢ per book in the U.S. and $1.25 per book in Canada.* I understand that accepting the 2 free books and gifts places me under no obligation to buy anything. I can always return a shipment and cancel at any time by calling the number below. The free books and gifts are mine to keep no matter what I decide.

Choose one: ☐ **Harlequin Special Edition**
(235/335 HDN GRJV) ☐ **Harlequin Heartwarming Larger-Print**
(161/361 HDN GRJV)

Name (please print)

Address   Apt. #

City   State/Province   Zip/Postal Code

Email: Please check this box ☐ if you would like to receive newsletters and promotional emails from Harlequin Enterprises ULC and its affiliates. You can unsubscribe anytime.

Mail to the **Harlequin Reader Service:**
IN U.S.A.: P.O. Box 1341, Buffalo, NY 14240-8531
IN CANADA: P.O. Box 603, Fort Erie, Ontario L2A 5X3

Want to try 2 free books from another series! Call 1-800-873-8635 or visit www.ReaderService.com.

*Terms and prices subject to change without notice. Prices do not include sales taxes, which will be charged (if applicable) based on your state or country of residence. Canadian residents will be charged applicable taxes. Offer not valid in Quebec. This offer is limited to one order per household. Books received may not be as shown. Not valid for current subscribers to the Harlequin Special Edition or Harlequin Heartwarming series. All orders subject to approval. Credit or debit balances in a customer's account(s) may be offset by any other outstanding balance owed by or to the customer. Please allow 4 to 6 weeks for delivery. Offer available while quantities last.

Your Privacy—Your information is being collected by Harlequin Enterprises ULC, operating as Harlequin Reader Service. For a complete summary of the information we collect, how we use this information and to whom it is disclosed, please visit our privacy notice located at corporate.harlequin.com/privacy-notice. From time to time we may also exchange your personal information with reputable third parties. If you wish to opt out of this sharing of your personal information, please visit readerservice.com/consumerschoice or call 1-800-873-8635. **Notice to California Residents**—Under California law, you have specific rights to control and access your data. For more information on these rights and how to exercise them, visit corporate.harlequin.com/california-privacy.

HSEHW22R3

COUNTRY LEGACY COLLECTION

19 FREE BOOKS IN ALL!

EMMETT
Diana Palmer

COURTED BY THE COWBOY

THE RANCHER AND THE BABY

Cowboys, adventure and romance await you in this
new collection! Enjoy superb reading all year long
with books by bestselling authors like
Diana Palmer, Sasha Summers and Marie Ferrarella!

YES! Please send me the **Country Legacy Collection!** This collection begins with
3 FREE books and 2 FREE gifts in the first shipment. Along with my 3 free books,
I'll also get 3 more books from the **Country Legacy Collection**, which I may either
return and owe nothing or keep for the low price of $24.60 U.S./$28.12 CDN each
plus $2.99 U.S./$7.49 CDN for shipping and handling per shipment*. If I decide to
continue, about once a month for 8 months, I will get 6 or 7 more books but will only
pay for 4. That means 2 or 3 books in every shipment will be FREE! If I decide to
keep the entire collection, I'll have paid for only 32 books because 19 are FREE!
I understand that accepting the 3 free books and gifts places me under no obligation
to buy anything. I can always return a shipment and cancel at any time. My free
books and gifts are mine to keep no matter what I decide.

☐ 275 HCK 1939   ☐ 475 HCK 1939

Name (please print)

Address   Apt. #

City   State/Province   Zip/Postal Code

Mail to the **Harlequin Reader Service:**
IN U.S.A.: P.O. Box 1341, Buffalo, NY 14240-8571
IN CANADA: P.O. Box 603, Fort Erie, Ontario L2A 5X3

*Terms and prices subject to change without notice. Prices do not include sales taxes, which will be charged (if applicable) based
on your state or country of residence. Canadian residents will be charged applicable taxes. Offer not valid in Quebec. All orders
subject to approval. Credit or debit balances in a customer's account(s) may be offset by any other outstanding balance owed by
or to the customer. Please allow 3 to 4 weeks for delivery. Offer available while quantities last. © 2021 Harlequin Enterprises ULC.
® and ™ are trademarks owned by Harlequin Enterprises ULC.

Your Privacy—Your information is being collected by Harlequin Enterprises ULC, operating as Harlequin Reader Service. To see
how we collect and use this information visit https://corporate.harlequin.com/privacy-notice. From time to time we may also exchange
your personal information with reputable third parties. If you wish to opt out of this sharing of your personal information, please
visit www.readerservice.com/consumerschoice or call 1-800-873-8635. Notice to California Residents—Under California law, you
have specific rights to control and access your data. For more information visit https://corporate.harlequin.com/california-privacy.

50BOOKCL22

COMING NEXT MONTH FROM
Love Inspired

PINECRAFT REFUGE
Pinecraft Seasons • by Lenora Worth

Grieving widower Tanner Dawson has no intentions of ever marrying again, but when he meets Eva Miller sparks fly. Giving her a job at his store is the last thing he wants, but he needs the help. As they get closer, can he keep his secrets to protect his daughter?

THE SECRET AMISH ADMIRER
by Virginia Wise

Shy Eliza Zook has secretly been in love with popular Gabriel King since they were children, but he has never noticed her. When a farm injury forces Gabriel to work alongside her in an Amish gift shop, will it be her chance to finally win him over?

REUNITED BY THE BABY
Sunset Ridge • by Brenda Minton

After finding a baby abandoned in the back of his truck, Matthew Rivers enlists the help of RN Parker Smythe, the woman whose love he once rejected. When their feelings start to blossom, could it lead them on a path to something more?

HER ALASKAN RETURN
Serenity Peak • by Belle Calhoune

Back in her hometown in Alaska, single and pregnant Autumn Hines comes face-to-face with first love Judah Campbell when her truck breaks down. Still reeling from tragedy, the widowed fisherman finds hope when he reconnects with Autumn. But can their relationship withstand the secret she's been keeping?

A HOME FOR THE TWINS
by Danielle Thorne

The struggling Azalea Inn is the perfect spot for chef Lindsey Judd to raise her twin boys. But things get complicated when lawyer Donovan Ainsworth comes to stay. Love is the last thing either of them want, but two little matchmakers might feel differently...

HIS TEMPORARY FAMILY
by Julie Brookman

Firefighter Sam Tiernan's life gets turned upside down when a car accident leaves his baby nieces in his care. When his matchmaking grandmother ropes next-door neighbor Fiona Shay into helping him, it might be the push they both need to open their hearts to something more...

LOOK FOR THESE AND OTHER LOVE INSPIRED BOOKS WHEREVER BOOKS ARE SOLD, INCLUDING MOST BOOKSTORES, SUPERMARKETS, DISCOUNT STORES AND DRUGSTORES.

LICNM0223